KAIN

Quest for the Lost Sword, Nebula

Told through the eyes of the villainous prince, Kain. A mischievous young man who knows nothing of love, cursed to be torn from his royal family at a very young age and separated from his twin brother, Abel. He is taken in by the cruel sorcerer, Ariaus who manipulates his mind into jealousy and hate. Abel, blessed by the God of Light, is left to rule his beautiful Kingdom while Kain, blessed by the God of Shadow, grows bitter over time, plotting his own brother's death. His malicious plans lead him on the greatest journey of his life as he discovers his mysterious past and meets a handsome knight named Leo.

Kain finds himself lost through his vast and magical world as he encounters many strange beings, including an old witch, who tells him of a sword he is destined to wield. With it, he can achieve the greatest power and unlock his darkest desires. Kain is left with only one choice but to challenge his most dangerous enemy, himself.

A story drawn together by erotic love, passion, intrigue, and redemption of the heart. Lessons are learned and choices are made between good and evil, love and power. Which path will he choose?

KAIN

Quest for the Lost Sword, Nebula

Written by
Ginger Anne London

Edited by Michela Dee and Jeffrey Boisvert

Author photo by Michela Dee

Cover art by Ginger Anne London

This book is dedicated
with love to

My fiancée, Michela Dee
Jeffrey Boisvert
Patricia Washburn
Kim Long and little Noah

And to my family,
who I love dearly and always will

Preface

I wrote Kain back in 1999. My writing has changed dramatically since then, but I wanted to share this story with you all either way. Before writing this book, I dreamed for there to be an LGBT related novel that was fantasy and adventure themed, but couldn't find it anywhere I searched. I wanted to write about a bisexual male character who was not a hero to begin with. This was difficult to find over ten years ago and only a few authors were writing books and film that had any gay themes at all. My love for fantasy, adventure, and sci-fi has always been with me since I was a child and I really wanted to help bring more of that into the LGBT community. I believe there should be more books for teenagers, young adults, and adults alike that enable the reader to escape reality into a fantasy or sci-fi world that does not always have a straight protagonist.

Kain to me is a part of myself that I wished I could have released back then. He is only one of the many characters that present the feelings I had. Each character plays a great role, expressing their personas that relate to so many. Kain is a man that is comfortable with his sexuality, with himself, and follows where his heart takes him. It is a strength that many of us lack or wish we could obtain in ourselves who struggle with our own sexuality and confidence. We must learn to accept, love ourselves, and be who we were born to be. If it is that you desire to be a male or female, then let that person you are living inside come out and love whoever it is you wish to love, no matter the sex. There is nothing greater than love in this world and it is what every human searches for, but does not always obtain. It is that precious of a gift and should be cherished, never denied, no matter what gender it is reflected within.

Kain's character knows nothing of love, like most of us starting out in life who have yet to find true love or understand the caring of others. Over time, this can reflect the darkness living inside some people who reject it, who ignore it, who believe it does not exist or that it can do nothing but make one weak. With Kain, I wanted to show the reader that is not true and what happens to those who grow bitter or alone is due to their own lack of faith. Remember, before others love you, you must first learn to love yourself.

Kain was a character that helped me get through the hardest times of my life. He helped to show me strength when my heart grew weak and to love myself, accept myself, and others will learn to accept me. I hope that Kain can do the same for you as he did for me and take you on a great journey across his world, make you smile and laugh with his flamboyant actions and colorful choices of words. When your life is acting a bit bumpy or rough, I want to take you away to a different place, let your mind be free, feel the butterfly feelings and just explore a world beyond our own. I want you to listen to the characters in the story, try to connect with them, understand them and let it be you who decide what path you would choose. Good and evil are within us all but it is really about where your heart can guide you that will tell you where you will end up. All of us control our own destiny and create our own paths. Be you, be unique, and shine like the stars you are.

-Ginger Anne London

Introduction

You may be wondering about who is telling this story. I would like to introduce myself. I am Kain and I am the prince of Tarot. My father passed away some time ago. I have a brother, my twin, who lives in the far lands beyond my country. I am quite tall and my hair is very long, slightly wavy, and black. I am thin, not overly muscular, but lean to the point of having a lovely build. My skin is the color of new milk and my eyes are a pale, icy blue colder than the glaciers of the northern mountains.

By the way, my plan is to kill my innocent, kind-hearted twin that protects our homeland from evil, powerful, dark souls…such as I. Someday, I wish to rule this world and I shall have every mortal being bow down to me.

You're probably saying to yourself, "Another twin brother story, where one wishes to kill the other for power?" Well, in a time of kings and queens, who *isn't* fighting for power?

Anyway, this story may seem like two brothers, one good and one wicked, battling each other out to the death. It turns out to be far different… you will see…I have no wish to spoil it for you. Sit back and... enjoy!

Chapter One
The Witch in the Tree

There was once a time when I walked throughout my darkened castle and wondered, "W*hy am I here*?" My mother was murdered when I was just a small boy. I was separated from my father and brother during a battle, then taken in by a powerful and wealthy being named Ariaus, who raised me in the kingdom of Tarot. Then, I was just a boy, ten years of age and very frightened.

I was taught much by my master, Ariaus. He was a powerful, magical being with many gifts to teach me. Ariaus said I was the chosen one of the Dark God, Sceptor. Sceptor is the strongest and most powerful of the malicious Gods. You could say he is pure evil. My master spoke to me about a lost sword called Nebula. It held the power that could make any mortal even more powerful than one of the Gods. Ariaus said I was destined to get my hands on this sword. If I do not, I can never rule this world.

I moved over to the tall, stained-glass window in my bed chamber and folded my arms across my chest. A lock of my raven hair fell in front of my eyes. I did not brush it aside. I was lost in the deep thoughts of getting this sword while my master was brewing a concoction in his potion room. I put two fingers on my chin as if to convey an intelligent visage. I stared out my lofty window, open to the cool breeze, and beheld all the land of Tarot, from the darkened forest to a small city of poor and filthy people.

My mind was filled with turmoil. "I must get out of here," I whispered to myself softly. I swiftly snatched my black velvet cloak and stalked down the dark, stone-walled stair. I told a servant that I passed to inform Ariaus that I went for a ride and would be back soon. I was in deep thought, and I was hoping I could see my brother, who believes, wrongly, that I am of no threat to him. I rode around the dark forest for a short time, though it seemed days.

As I approached the heart of the forest, I saw a shadowy tree, huge, with a hole at the base. I saw movement in the shadows. I stopped to see if anything was living in this enormous tree. I unsheathed my sword and pointed it directly at its thick trunk. Leaping off the back of Mage, my trusty black horse, I gazed quietly into the dark hole, which was about the size of a dwarf. Then, as I was starting to believe there was nothing there, I turned my back and walked away. I was beginning to mount my horse when I heard a voice.

"What is it you seek, young man?" The voice spoke with an aged, irritable tone. I turned quickly, pointing my sword at the creature. It was an old woman, a stout crone that looked as if she had lived within the darkness of this forest for centuries. I raised my eyebrow and stared at her with my pale eyes. She was filthy and looked much like the dirt on which I was standing.

"Ha, you are silenced by my wizened face young man, no?" The old woman said, this time laughing softly to herself while she stared back at me. I could not stand the sight of her, nor the scent, and I only wished to leave this place.

"You should not judge me, young man, when you know nothing of me. I know you want answers to many questions ....those, I can give," she stared at me and I felt ensnared by her presence. I felt as if I could not move. Was she reading my thoughts?

"Do you know who I am, woman?" I inquired in a deep tone of voice, charmingly, but with an edge of unspoken warning.

"Of course I know who you are. I know everything about you, handsome one," she replied. I watched her move toward my horse as she began to pat him. I did not want her to touch him, for the Gods knew what she held that could sicken him.

"Do not touch him, crone! Now be gone from my sight and my nose! I wish nothing of you. I am leaving your filthy tree hole and your dirt-eaten face!" I shouted. She began to laugh and moved silently away from Mage, who was whinnying with agitation. I raised my eyebrow once more and wondered what treachery this old woman had planned.

"Are you mocking me, woman?" I snapped. She continued to laugh and I glowered at her in silence. I pointed my sword at her and said, "How dare you laugh at me! I shall kill you for your mockery!"

"You need my help, young man! I suggest you move that thing away from my face... and listen to what I have to say," she stated, staring at me with her green, corrupt eyes. She twitched her hand and pointed to an area directly behind her tree.

"Please sit with me by the fire," she invited, gesturing to an encampment. Inexplicably, I did as she wished. There were two, small, wooden seats to either side of a tiny rock circle that was filled with fresh, dry kindling. I wondered about the two seats and the fire pit; it was as if she was expecting me to sit with her hours before I arrived. I watched her every move for I could not take chances with this old woman. She began building a fire while looking up at me. I crossed my legs and sat in a distinguished manner, relaxed, yet in control. My hair was tied back with a velvet ribbon that was beginning to come undone. Pieces of my raven locks now lay in front of my eyes, making me look quite insane.

"Your beauty is striking, young man. You hold a power within you: a very strong, amazing power with skills given to you by the dark God Sceptor." She continued to stare at me with her dark small eyes.

I looked back at her and whispered in a soft tone, "I have a power...by the dark God Sceptor? What power is this, old hag?" My eyebrows came together while I stared at her. My ears waited for her to answer with her creaky old voice.

"This power is very strong. It is the gift to using your mind to do many things. No human can do this without the power you hold. This ability can enable you to make flames within the palm of your hand, talk to animals, plants, and spirits that you could never dream of without it. You can hear things that others will never sense. More importantly, conjure forces others could never even dream of, no matter how much they tried. Do you understand me, young man?" She explained gravely, waving her wrinkly hands slowly above the flame.

I stared at her for a moment, my eyes wide with shock. At first I did not believe her, but I remember Ariaus saying long ago that I was the chosen one. So what if the old woman meant what she said? I must speak to Ariaus about this before I do anything else. I picked up my head and looked back at the old woman that was staring into her pitiful fire

"So, this power I have… is there a limit? I mean... is it more powerful than the God or just as powerful as they are?" I inquired. She stood up from her seat and picked up a wooden staff with a feather tied to the tip. She walked around the fire and began laughing to herself.

"Young man, the power is not less or more than any God. It is a gift from the dark deity to help guide you to your destiny. It is not until you find your fate that you become most powerful in all the world. Don't you see, young man? The power is deep within you in order to help you get through your life and complete your mission. Such a mission... that the dark God... has chosen for you," she croaked. She began dancing then laughing to herself again. I watched her, but at the same time, I was thinking just what about she was talking about. She then stopped laughing and came very close, pointing her nose inches away my face. Her eyes were dark, but the fire reflected brightly within them.

"There is something else I wish to tell you. You are not the only one with this gift. There is one other who is blessed as you are. His power is far greater than yours and can destroy you if desired. This ability is not handed down to the other by the dark God, but instead by the God of light." She stared at the fire, moving back to her seat. I watched her, losing all feeling in my body.

"Who is this other person? Is he mortal? Should I fear this person? Answer me, woman!" I snapped. My eyes darkened and my brows came down, making me look more *evil* than I already looked. She laughed in response.

"Ha ha... young man, how I wish I could tell you, but this is something you need to discover on your own. It is getting late and soon the moon will rise for the creatures of the night," she spoke poetically. The dusk was indeed falling I knew I should head back to the castle before master Ariaus became worried. I looked up at the sky and looked back at the old woman.

"Thank you for your help, but indeed you are right. It is getting late and I must be off," I whispered softly to her, standing up from the meager wooden seat. I picked out a few gold pieces from the coin purse at my hip and gave them to her. I watched her smile at me, revealing her dirty green teeth, I turned my back and exited the campsite, jumping back up on my steed, who was waiting for me, then rode off back to the castle.

Chapter two
A Brotherly Visit

When I arrived at the castle, I hung up my cloak and marched swiftly up the stone staircase to see my master. I was very tired and wished to speak with him before going off to bed. I folded my arms and walked into the parlor. There was a large fire roaring in the fireplace with an inviting armchair directly in front of it. I was hoping to have a seat and relax. When I got closer, I was startled by a deep, aged man's voice.

"Where have you been, Kain?"

I spotted Ariaus who was sitting in the arm chair, arms crossed, with an expression of displeasure crossing his lips. I walked over to him and knelt at his feet. I looked at him with my innocent, yet charming eyes. My lashes were long and dark, my face was pure and pale, my lips, moist, bore the most charming hint of rose hue.

"Master, I went riding and met an old dwarf woman that lived in a tree," I exclaimed. He stared at me, though his face was covered in a dark shadow. I saw his long, white hand come out to touch the side of my face.

"You are so beautiful, you do things that infuriate me, but how can I be angry at you? You, who I was told to protect and teach," he sighed and began stroking my face softly. Oh, how I loved it when he did. I bowed my head, overwhelmed by the warmth of his touch, and no words managed to come from my mouth. It was as if he had me under a spell, preventing me from speaking. He touched my bottom lip with his thumb. "Did I not say to speak to no one…in these forests?" He whispered softly to me, like silk in my ear. I looked up at him and then back down again. I did remember him telling me such things, but of course I never listened to him.

"Master, I am sorry. Please do not be angry with me." I touched his hand that stroked my face, and then slid his hand over my lips so I may kiss it. His skin was cold, but very soft. I thought I heard a bit of soft laughter from him.

"Dear boy, I am not angry at you. What I do wish to know is what did this woman say to you?" He inquired. I looked back at him and continued to hold his hand.

"She said she knew everything about me. She said I held a special power that was given to me by the dark God," I responded breathlessly. He spoke no words, but instead, his face was hidden from me. I could not tell what expression was on his face.
"Master? Is this true, what the old woman said? Was I given such a power?" I asked insistently.
He came closer to me, leaning over to place his head into the light of the fire. I stared at him and his features, how his eyebrows were thick, but perfectly shaping his dark eyes that were richly hued with a true blue. His face was pale with few lines in it. His white hair was long and hanging over his shoulders. He was old, but his appearance did not show his true age. He was quite attractive for a man like him and he carried a deep, but soothing voice.

"Kain my dear boy, you were not supposed to know this until the time was right, but then again, why not now? I do believe perhaps now would be the time to teach you," He laughed softly to himself. "Why have I been waiting? I guess I have not noticed how much you have grown in the past years." He moved his lips over to my cheek and kissed it softly. I felt his warm breath and soft lips against my cold cheek and it sent goose bumps throughout my body. He stared at me while I shivered, noticing that my eyes were softly closed. I opened them in response.

"You are not angry with me master?" I asked innocently.

He smiled with his perfect white teeth and softly said, "Not at all my dear boy, not at all." I watched him stand up from the chair and I, still kneeling on the ground, stood up as well. I, in a way had not wanted him to move from that chair, for I enjoyed his presence immensely. It was warm and comfortable. I could have stayed there with him all night. He walked over to a mirror on the wall in the same room and began lighting a small candle next to it. The candle was placed in a holder with a handle and he noticed I was watching him with a smile. He beamed at me and then spoke across the large marble room.

"Good night, beautiful one. We shall speak more about this in the morning." He turned his back and walked up the stairs that lead him to his bed chamber. I stood there alone, folding my arms and looking at the fireplace. I walked over to the armchair and sat down in it, leaning my elbow on the arm of the chair.

I sat and stared at the fireplace. The Gods only knew how long I was there. I noticed myself staring and began thinking of my brother. I forgot all about seeing him when I met the old woman in the forest. *I will set off tomo*rrow, I decided, *but before I do that, I must tell master Ariaus. I do hope he does not mind, though he never minds when I travel.* I got up from the chair, walked up the stairs to my bed chamber and took off my clothes. I climbed into bed and watched the bright, full moon from my large window. I fell softly to sleep, dreaming of the power I had within me.

When I had awakened, I heard Ariaus' voice throughout the castle. He was demanding one of the servants to kill a rat that was loose in his room of chemicals and magic. That was Ariaus' chamber where he studied the black arts. I hardly ever bothered him when he was busy in that room, for the Gods only knew what went on down there. He had noticed I was awake and turned towards me, smiling, and yelled to me across the room as usual.

"Good morning Prince Kain." He said to me in a very happy manner, as if he could not wait till I had awoken. I was standing on the stairs, watching him. My hair was not tied back, but instead it hung over my shoulders with spiral curls. I had put my black sleeved shirt on and matching leather paints before leaving my room, of course. My belt and sword were not yet attached to my trousers and I had my black leather vest over my puffy-sleeved shirt. I felt very powerful, although very *evil.*

Why do I like to feel this way? Is it right for me to feel this way? I had always thought of such things. I wear the color of death, though my brother wore the colors of the rainbow. Why was this so? Oh well, it did not matter, for black was a lovely shade to me. I noticed there was a mirror off to the right hand side of me and I looked in it. *My Gods! Did I look like some angel? Is this what everyone means when they call me the beautiful one?* I smiled in the mirror and a sparkle twinkled upon my teeth as I continued to descend the steps. I strode elegantly over to Ariaus, who was wondering where the rat could have gone. He heard me walking up to him and turned around to face me. It seemed he stared at me for hours, but it was only for a second. I smiled at him.

"Did you sleep well, master?" I askcd cheerfully.

"Yes indeed I did... my boy!" He exclaimed, smiling back at me.

He began laughing softly to himself as he put his arm around my shoulder and walked me over to our grand dining table.

"Come, have breakfast with me," said he. I loved it when he was in a good mood. I smiled and walked over with him and he pulled out a seat for me to sit. The servant had poured us some coffee, which I adored. I looked over at Ariaus and sipped my beverage.

"Master, I plan to set forth on a journey to see my brother today. Is that all right with you?" I asked. He looked at me and smiled.

"Of course it's all right with me. I was planning to teach you how to use your inner power, but if you wish to see him, I accept that. I know how you love to tease him," he calmly replied. He chuckled to himself again while staring at me and sipping his coffee. I loved talking to him, for he always knew how to soothe me.

After breakfast, I fetched my cloak and put my belt on with my sword attached. I walked up to the door and wished Ariaus well. I went outside and jumped on Mage, listening to the birds sing the morning away. I did love the daybreak, though one would think I would love the night even more. I rode off through the dark woods and over the flatlands. I adored the plains, for you could ride as fast as the wind, yet never be tired of it. Mage can ride swiftly; he is a robust steed. If I were a horse, I would be him.

I reached a small village directly outside of Tarot. I stopped to rest in a dim, lantern-lit tavern and watched everyone stare at me. I could hear them whispering about me, but I could not understand what they were saying. I remembered what the old woman said about my power and how I can hear things that others could never hear. At this moment, I wished I could hear what they were saying. I tried to focus my power on them, but I knew nothing of how to use it. I laughed to myself, walking over to a table and sitting down, crossing my legs. A tall man walked over to me and asked me if I wanted something. I looked up at him with my bright, ice blue eyes.

"Yes, please do get me a glass of red wine, sir," I ordered. The man walked away for a minute to get my drink. While he did that, a short and dirty looking young boy came up to me, wearing nothing but rags.

"Are you Prince Abel?" Said the boy innocently. He looked up to me as if I were a God. I felt somewhat bad for him, though my brain was telling me to shoo him away.

"No…I am not prince Abel. I am his twin brother, Kain. He looked at me rather disappointedly and then looked down again as he walked away from me. At this point, everyone was obviously staring at me and I was beginning to feel quite uncomfortable. I wanted to leave, but then again, I loved the attention. I looked at everyone right back with my impossibly light eyes and the tall man returned with my drink. I sat there, sipping my wine, remarking to myself that people have no manners to stare at others as they do. Shortly after, my glass was empty. I put a gold coin down on the wooden table and stood up from my chair.

Though I was not completely rested from the long ride, I decided to vacate. I walked out of the tavern and hopped on my horse. I continued to ride out of the small village and rode over the hills and onward toward my home town. This was the village of Bane. Bane was a beautiful, enchanted place that my brother ruled over as prince. My brother is very powerful and is known to be a very good sword fighter during battle. Now of course I was jealous of him and wished him dead for being more powerful than I. Then again now, with this inner power I might be able to defeat Abel, take over

Bane, then soon thereafter…the world. I rode up to the castle walls, which were guarded by gallant knights. I hopped off my horse and walked up to one of the armor-clad men.

"Let me pass! I am the prince's brother," I proclaimed.

The knights looked at each other and bowed to me, then opened the gates. I hopped back on Mage and we rode through the immense castle garden. There was the entrance to the massive castle, built of gleaming white stone. I jumped off Mage and the guards saw who I was as they opened the door to the great hall for me. I walked in, my feet echoing on the marble floor of the massive chamber, and there was my twin brother, sitting on his throne. He and I were identical, save for the color of our hair. His mane was a shining golden blonde and mine gleamed in a shimmering black. I grinned at him, slowly revealing my polished teeth as I walked up to him. Minstrels were playing elegant melodies on the upper level of the hall and curious eyes stared at me in bewilderment from each side, but I did not dare turn my head from my brother. I then saw him look up and he noticed I had entered. I could have just killed him right there, but he seemed too joyous to see me. His eyes widened and a huge smile came across his face.

"Brother! My goodness, it's been years! Where have you been? I have missed you and hope that you come to live with me. Have you gotten any of my letters?" He asked.

"Yes, it has and no, I haven't," I replied in a monotone.

"What? That's odd; I've been sending them to you for years! Lately, the surrounding villages have been struggling and I've been begging for you to return home and help me rule this kingdom!" He declared. "And you say you have not received even one?"

"I have not received any letters from you, brother, so the answer is no," I responded coldly. He looked shocked for a moment, but then put his arms on my shoulders and kissed me. He loved to do this and adored seeing me after a long time. His dream was for me and him to rule this kingdom hand-in-hand. *As if I would*, I thought, for I was too greedy and filled with jealousy for him. Why would I do such a thing? He stared at me and I stared directly back at him. He and I were mirror images, but he was not so dark and devilish looking as I was. I bore a look that sucked in the darkness around me, while he in turn absorbed the light. He radiated a glow, while I faded off into the darkness. It was strange seeing us together. I was envious of him, I admit it.

He treasured me so, yet I hated him for it. I despised how he could love me, who was so filled with resentment for him. I kissed him on his cheek and he shivered with shock, but I knew he enjoyed it. He then pulled me close to him and drew me into a warm embrace. I watched behind his back members of the court and knights gazing at us. Servants stared at how much we looked alike. Everyone was silent until Prince Abel told them to speak. They respected him and followed his every command. He made everyone happy and the village was filled with riches. There were no poor, no sick without care, no filth, only wealth and prosperity. I wanted what he had! I wanted it all! Abel, after holding me for several minutes, escorted me over to the dinner table. He told everyone to come and enjoy the feast with him.

"Come, everyone! Tonight there is going to be a feast to welcome my brother, Kain!" He joyfully announced. When he was finished with his speech, the townspeople and attendants sat around the enormous stone table before the throne. The castle was filled with inviting heat emanating from the crowd and lit torches. Food was brought out to the table. There were all kinds of roasted meats, vegetables grown in the farms of the surrounding lands, breads with a sumptuous variety of flavors, rich desserts, and all the spirits the kingdom could drink. I stared at everyone feasting and enjoying themselves and I noticed there was a man skulking off in the distance in a dark corner. He was leaning up against the wall with his arms crossed against his chest, loosely grasping a brass goblet of mead. His hair was short and black in the back, but his bangs were very long, reaching past his nose and covering his eyes. His face was pale white and his lips were stained with a tint of red wine and perfectly plump. He looked quite muscular and his eyes, I noticed where I was sitting, were bright green, like a cat's eye. His face was square and exuded the appearance of strength. He had a chiseled jaw and he was dressed entirely in black leather. He was drinking sweet red honey wine, but not eating.

My eyes were drawn specifically to him. He noticed that I was staring at him and turned his head slightly to the right, as if to pretend not to notice me. I bit a piece of my chicken as my brother touched my shoulder. He kept pulling me close to him, excitedly sharing tales to me of the battles he fought. I pretended I was listening to him and smiled at everything he was saying, but truthfully I wanted to know who that *man* was, for there was something about him I liked. When my brother was finished eating and telling his stories, I whispered to him and pointed out the dark figure leaning up against the wall.

“Abel, who is that man?” I asked inquisitively. My brother then laughed, revealing his bright ivory teeth. *Oh how charming he looked when he laughed. Is this what I look like when I laugh?* I wondered. He then smiled at me.

"Why my dear brother, that is Sir Leo. He is my strongest knight and quite handsome too," he replied exuberantly. He chuckled again while beaming at me and took another sip of his wine. I grinned slyly at him with one eyebrow pointing upwards. He was attractive and filled with that damn bright glow. In a way you could say I wanted to love him back as he loved me. I desired to be his true brother, but something inside me stopped me from doing this. Was it my greedy need to be the most powerful? Yes, perhaps it was, but who can say that they would not want to be the most powerful in the world? Well, I had noticed that Sir Leo had moved from his spot and I got up from my seat. My brother noticed that I had stood from the table.

"Where is it you go to, my brother?" He inquired. He looked at me with the same innocent eyes I give to Ariaus. I gazed at him with a soft expression.

"I am just going for a walk, Abel. I shall return soon. Do you mind?" I replied, touching the side of his cheek, then his chin, and I grinned down at him. I was doing exactly what Ariaus did to me when I give him those eyes of purity. At that moment I felt like Ariaus. He shivered at my touch, took my hand, and kissed it.

"Of course I do not mind, my brother. Please do explore the castle. You remember where your bed chamber is, right?" He said with a kind expression. I then grinned, showing my teeth, and whispered to him while touching his lip with my thumb.

"Indeed I do, my brother, indeed I do," I responded sensuously. I smiled at him one more time then wandered away from the feast and into one of the castle's many rooms. There were torches all around the walls revealing paintings and tapestries the size of the wall itself.

I must give it to my brother for he has good taste, I remarked to myself. I walked around the rooms in search of that knight, Sir Leo. I had wandered throughout the castle it seemed for hours until I heard faint footsteps behind me, following my every move. I looked on the wall to see if there was a shadow behind me and saw nothing. I continued to walk down the corridors and I found myself in a dark, but enchantingly large room with a fireplace lit with a roaring flame to relax in after the long walk. I decided to sit in a large, brilliantly carved wooden chair with cherubs sculpted in elegant detail all around it. It was beautiful and I thought of perhaps asking my brother if I could have it.

Thinking of this, I laughed to myself. I was then startled by a hand that touched my shoulder from behind me. I turned my head very quickly and noticed a dark figure standing above me. It was Sir Leo leaning there with his dark eyes and long bangs in front of his face. My Gods, how beautiful he looked. All I could do was gawk at him his large hand that was beautifully rugged, certainly the product of wielding his sword through many glorious battles. The color of his skin was the same pallor as mine. I stood up, staring at him, and felt his robust hand slide off my shoulder. It gave me goose bumps. I noticed my eyes closed when I felt this and then I opened them right after the feeling. He stood there in silence, staring at me. I then heard a sweet, deep, calm voice from him.

"You look identical to your brother. Do you notice this?" He whispered silkily. My Gods, I was melting when he spoke. I was so lost in him that I could not say anything at all. I looked to the side of me to stop myself from drowning in the overwhelming sensation.

"Yes I do notice that, my friend," I responded breathlessly. He just stared up and down at me in disbelief that I looked so much like him. I noticed him approaching me, closer to the fireplace to see me better. I then could see every detail about him. He had an irresistible aura surrounding him that pulled any unsuspecting man or woman nearer to him. He looked innocent, but also strong and polite. I then noticed he took my hand and very slowly kissed it, getting down on one knee. I do believe I almost fainted at this moment until I heard his voice say in a velvety tone, "I am Sir Leo, my prince."

I could have kissed him right there, but instead, I began to feel angry, annoyed that my brother is surrounded by the most chivalrous people. *Not fair at all!* I whined to myself, fighting the blush from spreading across my cheeks. I stared at him holding my hand and I did not want him to stop.

"Do you know my true name, Sir Leo?" I asked teasingly.

He looked at me and placed my hand back down to my side.

"Yes, of course I do," he replied, "You are Prince Kain. I know somewhat of the story between you and your brother. Prince Abel always speaks highly of you and I could not wait to one day meet you."

I could not believe that he could not wait to see me. *Me, who is cruel and evil? Me, who wishes to destroy my brother for power! Why? Well, perhaps I must hide my greedy side well, for others who want to meet me,* I laughed to myself, bowing my head. Sir Leo then looked at me, wondering why I was chuckling.

"Prince Kain, why is it that you laugh?" He inquired.

I looked at him and whispered, "Nothing, charming one…" I then looked at him, smiling with my handsome allure. He beamed and I do believe I spied him blushing a bit. I raised my eyebrow and thought to myself, my smile turning into a grin. *I wonder if I could take him back with me to my castle?* I began laughing to myself again and Sir Leo stared at me and shook his head in amusement.

"My Prince, I do believe you love to laugh," he remarked.

I looked at him, feeling entertained, and said kindly, "Yes, indeed I do, Sir Leo, indeed I do." He then bowed before me, kissing my hand again and said, "My prince, I must go. Perhaps I will see you tomorrow?" I did not want him to go, but it was getting late and I knew he wanted to go to bed.

"Yes, perhaps I will see you tomorrow. Goodnight, Sir Leo." I said to him with a sweet smile.

"Goodnight my prince," he whispered in return. I saw him turn his back and walk into the next room. What a graceful stride he had as well. He had to have also been blessed by the Gods. I found myself back to the feast and by this time, everyone was drunk and tired. I looked for Abel, but he was not there.

I whispered to myself, "I wonder where he is?" I went upstairs to see maybe if he was up in his bedchamber. I came to a very long hallway and I walked all the way down to the end of it. The walls were lined with torches leading all the way down. At the end, there were carved angels on each side guarding a very large door. How beautiful he kept this castle. I touched the carvings of cherubs and roses sculpted within the wood of the door, which were painted in gold and decorated with red velvet. I looked within the crack of the door and saw a light from within. I knocked softly and heard my brother answer.

"Yes? What is it?"

I laid my head on the door and said, "It's me, your brother, Kain." Before I knew it, the door was opened. I looked at him, dressed in a white puffy shirt. The chest area was opened and not tied together. His hair was falling apart from the loose ribbon that was tied around it. He was wearing tight black paints and he wore a necklace with a purple stone on it around his neck with many gold rings on his fingers. Pieces of his hair were hanging in front of his eyes and he almost looked unkempt, like a madman. He smiled at me, grabbing my arm, and pulled me in the room.

"Where have you been my brother? I looked all over the castle for you," he remarked. He was still smiling at me as he shut the door. He did look exactly like me and it was in a way quite scary. I looked down and answered his question, almost forgetting that he asked.

"I only went for a walk my brother and I ran into Sir Leo," I stated.

I saw my brother grin at me and he touched the side of my cheek. "I see. Isn't he a charming one, Kain? Do not tell me he did not draw you into him," he said to me with a bit of laughter.

I smiled and knew how much he was right. My brother then took me over to his very large bed that could fit twelve men on it. I giggled at the absurd size. He set me down on an ornate chair that was upholstered in scarlet-hued velvet and sat down next to me. I looked over at the fireplace that was decorated with the same style of angels and cherubs as the hallway beyond. When I looked back, I noticed that he was staring at me with this strange smile on his face. He touched my cheek and turned my head until our eyes met.

"I love you, my brother. I have always loved you and I shall always continue to," he whispered softly. He moved closer to me and kissed me affectionately on my cheek. My eyes were still closed and my lips were parted slightly. I pushed myself away from him subtly. He was staring at me still, beaming, and blushing faintly.

I sensed his love for me and how I felt so terrible about myself. I was a monster compared to him and his loving heart. I, who wished to kill him and he was completely unaware. *My Gods, what do I do? I no longer wish to end his life. I forgot how much he loves me. I hate him for what he has, but he makes up for it by loving me. What kind of monster am I?* I thought, outraged with myself. I lowered my head and moved away from him. He moved closer and wrapped his arm around me, beginning to slide his fingers through my hair.

"What is wrong, Kain? You seem very sad and I hate when you are feeling down," he said to me in my ear in a soft tone. I had to get away from him, for I was beginning to feel ashamed for my cruel thoughts. I did not even notice the warm tears that began to stream down my face. He touched my chin and moved my head up to his.

"Do not cry Kain, please," He cooed sympathetically. He was kind and I was horrible. I wanted him to stop being sweet to me and to stop loving me… or did I? He wiped my tears away and kissed my cheek. I did not want him to stop, but at the same time, I did.

"Lay down, Kain, for maybe you need rest. Here, lay down," he said.

He laid me down on his supremely comfortable bed. I did not want to at first, but I found it difficult to resist as my head hit his fluffy feather pillows. What did I really want? I lay down and tried to refuse.

"No…please...no... I do not want to. Please no, Abel." I pleaded, but did as he asked; his pillows were plush and his bed was inviting. He lay down next to me and was still sliding his fingers through my hair. I loved it when he did that. He held my hand, continuing to kiss my cheek comfortingly. I do not remember much afterward, for I do believe I fell asleep listening to his voice. He put me to sleep with his soothing words of love.

Chapter Three
Emotions Reign

I woke up the next morning to bright daylight streaming in through large windows. I felt a hand across my chest move and noticed there were a few golden curls on my chest as well. I looked to the left of me and there lay my brother. He looked like an angel sleeping next to me. How beautiful he was with his glow and the sun touching his hair and face. His hand was soft and quite feminine with longer fingernails than most men. His hand began to slide across my chest. I felt him push himself closer to me and I even thought I felt his lips against my ear.

"I love you," I heard him whisper.

I moved my head slightly to the left, trying to see him. I felt locked and how I wanted to love him. Yes, I wanted to.

"I love you, Abel. I love you…" I whispered back to him, kissing his cheek. This could not be me, the one filled with anger; the one filled with evil and hate. I kept on saying it, "I love you. I love you. I love you." I found myself in bed, saying these words aloud. I opened my eyes and I saw Abel staring down at me with a huge smile. He was trying to wake me up. My Gods! I was dreaming! I was wondering if I said "I love you" out loud and if he heard it. I looked at Abel and felt strange. I did not know what to think. Did he hear what I was saying to him in the dream?

"I see you have dreams of someone you love, my brother?" He asked me with the kindest of words. I did not know what to say.

"Was I saying things out loud, Abel? What was I saying?" I inquired, looking at him and remembering how I held him in the dream. I was for sure losing my mind. He laughed charmingly.

"My brother, all you said was 'I love you' over and over. There must be a lady in your life, no?" He continued to laugh.

A lady? Me? What woman would put up with me? I began to laugh to myself. I saw him laughing with me and he kissed me on my cheek. I thought of what I said in the dream, that I loved him. Did I love him? Did I actually love him with all my heart? Well, it was just a dream. I laughed to myself again and rose out of bed. Like in the dream, the sun was shining in on the room and lit it up in all its beauty. I then heard my brother's voice off in the distance.

"My servants have made breakfast, dear brother. Do wish to eat?" He announced. I noticed I was still in my clothes from the previous night. I looked around the room and saw that my brother was nude in a dark corner. I stared at him and realized his body was exactly like mine. He was putting on some new clothes. He noticed that I was staring at him and walked closer to me, watching me gawk at him in response. He continued to put on his trousers no more than a few inches away from me. I could feel his breath against my face.

"What is it, my brother? Why do you stare at me so?" He asked curiously. I wanted to hug him and tell him I love him, but I knew it could not happen. He beamed.

"Nothing, my brother, It's just…." I stammered. I did not know what to say to him. I felt like something had started to change within me. I wanted to tell him that he was radiant and that I wanted to hold him. Suddenly, as if he was reading my thoughts, he slid his arms around my waist and pulled me close to him. He hugged me tightly and kissed my cheek softly. I closed my eyes, pulling him close to me as well and kissed his cheek back. He was shocked, for I never pulled him close and kissed him before. He pulled away from me slowly and began to laugh.

"You are such a pleasure to have with me. Please come downstairs and enjoy breakfast," He said. He took his long-nailed index finger and slowly touched my nose, smiling all the while.

"I would love to, my brother," I replied. He smiled and took my hand, kissing it. He then turned his back and walked over to the gold-framed mirror on the wall. He began taking his hair out of the ribbon that held it together. I leaned up against the wall, watching him, for this is what I do when I am home and waking up in the morning. His hair fell long past his shoulders, his curls golden, collecting and reflecting rays of light like that of an angel. He brushed out his hair slowly and then grabbed a blue ribbon that hung on the mirror. He tied his hair back gently, not too tightly. He kept wispy bangs in front of his eyes. He put on a blue velvet vest with gold embroidery lining the hems. He looked gorgeous in blue, for it made the color in his hair look more radiant. He put on a pair of black leather boots and attached his sword and sheath to his belt.

The way he dressed was elegant and precise. All clothing pieces matched harmoniously to make him practically glow with beauty. He sprayed an elegant fragrance from a sapphire-hued bottle and came up to me again, kissing my cheek.

"Now, come, my brother. Come with me," Abel said with purpose. He took my hand and led me downstairs to an ornately carved wooden table that was set for a breakfast. Every detail, from the table itself to the tiniest piece of elegant silverware, bore a glow from the sunlight streaming in from the window. His castle was like a palace in the clouds. His servants were dressed neatly in well-fitted tunics and dresses in Abel's uniform blue and gold. There were flowers everywhere, hanging all around walls and around the table. Even the scent of the room was fresh and lovely. I smelled coffee and food along with fresh bread. It was only my brother and I there to share the meal, no one else.

On the ceiling were painted images of angels in a cerulean sky. It was like nothing I had ever seen before. Out the windows, I could see a garden filled with statues of angels. I do believe my brother was obsessed with these magical beings with wings. I laughed at the thought, for my castle is adorned with gargoyles and demons, dark looking creatures with veiny, bat-like wings. How different were the things I saw there. I felt my brother take my hand and lead me over to a chair.

"Are you going to sit down and enjoy the food or stare at the walls all day?" He quipped, beginning to laugh. I smiled at him, for what he said was quite funny to me. I sat down and sipped some of the delicious coffee.

"Did you sleep well, Kain?" He inquired. I raised an eyebrow and thought of the dream.

"Oh, yes, I slept just wonderfully. Thank you," I replied.

He smiled at me with complete charm, as I did back to him as he ate the feast that was placed in front of us. My Gods, not only did the food smell delicious, but the taste far exceeded quality of the scent. I wanted this breakfast to last forever. I knew that today was the day I was planning on leaving and going back home, for it was the time for master Ariaus to teach me how to use my power. I looked at my brother now with no smile on my face. I was surprisingly quite sad that I had to be the one to tell him I was leaving.

"Abel?" I asked with a hint of nervousness in my voice.

"Yes, my beautiful brother?" he responded with that gorgeous smile of his.

"I shall be returning home today," I admitted. As I spoke, he looked up and dropped his fork.

"You are leaving? You have not even stayed for more than two days! Why so soon, my brother? Why?" His eyebrows came down over his eyes and he looked dejected and angry at the same time. I felt terrible that I had to leave him. I had changed dramatically since I first came here. What happened to me? Ariaus will identify this change as soon as I get home. What will become of me?

"I made plans to leave today. My master Ariaus expects me to return and I do not wish to keep him worrying. I shall leave after breakfast. Do not mistake me, my brother. I do wish I could stay here with you forever, but I must return," I explained.

He stared at me with his mouth so that his bottom teeth were visible. His eyes bore the expressions of sadness and shock. He sat back in his chair and darkness began to cover his gaze. He rested his arm on the side of the chair. His legs were crossed in the same way mine were and he closed his eyes to fight the onslaught of tears.

"All right… as you wish….you do not have to feel trapped here….you may leave whenever you wish…I can understand that," He stammered in a choked voice, resisting the urge to weep. I thought for a moment that the castle became dark. I saw the servants running to the windows. I looked behind me and discovered it had begun to rain outside. The servants were shutting the windows as swiftly as possible while a shadow covered my brother's face. Thunder cracked outside of the window.

How will I depart in this rain? I thought to myself. Nevertheless, the birds still cheeped and whistled. My brother rose from his chair and quickly exited the room. I watched him leave, knowing that he must be angry. I found it unusual. In fact, everything around me felt strange. I got up from my chair and ran into the next room, where it was completely dark. The only light in the room came from the large window in the corner.

Underneath was an armchair where my brother was seated. I walked up to him quietly and he seemed to not hear me. Was he pretending? I walked very close to him, standing behind as he watched the rain fall out the window. I touched his shoulder and whispered, "Abel, did I anger or sadden you?" He did not move nor speak, but continued to stare out the window. Then, I heard his voice.

"How can you leave me so soon? For years and years I waited for you and could not wait to see you again… and now this? You stay for one night and then wish to leave. I am sure Ariaus will understand if you stay longer. Do you not care about me or my feelings to leave me so soon?" He exclaimed.

I stood there and did not know what to say. He was right, for at the beginning, I did not seem to care much about him. I made plans to see him and leave as soon as possible. I looked down and he was getting annoyed, for I did not answer him. I wanted to tell him that I loved him. I wanted to kiss him, but I could not find the strength. I was not as strong as my brother. He let his feelings out openly like no one else in the world. That was the difference between me and him.

"Leave me Kain, for now I know the truth of you," He exclaimed, irate. My eyebrows came together and I began to feel lost.

"No Abel, that is not true. Please do not hate me for this. I am sorry!" I yelled. He got up from his chair and turned to face me. He was so filled with rage that I could feel it. I saw evil within his eyes and I started to wonder if I was him or he was me. Was it evil or was his anger making him appear to be temporarily malicious?

"Kain, I love you, do you not see that? I know everything about you! I know what you were born for! I know what you are to bring into this world! I never listened to anyone that told me. I continued to love you! I continued to be your brother no matter how I was warned about you! I told anyone who doubted you that I had to see for myself this evil within you! I now see that you care nothing for me and that what the elders have said is true! It's all true!" He shouted, bursting into tears. Seeing the tears pouring down his face, I wanted to kill myself at this moment. I wanted to take my sword out and stab myself through the heart. I was even plotting to kill him not even a day ago, but something broke free within me that I could not explain last night.

He knows of my evil? He knew all along that I hated him, but he did not believe it? He knew about my destiny? How can this be? I thought with the feeling of humiliation sinking through the pit of my stomach. I felt more ashamed than ever, for the only one who truly loved me had grown to hate me. It hurt, I must admit it that it hurt.

"Abel, please do not think I hate you. Please, Abel" I pleaded, trying desperately to get through to him. He stood from his spot and pushed me over to the door with strength I never thought he could possess.

"Get out, Kain! You are no longer my brother!" He screamed, enraged.

I was so shocked that I could not believe what he was saying. I wanted to cry, hold him, and tell him the truth. I wanted to, but I couldn't. What was wrong with me?

"No, Abel, please!" A tear began to fall from my eye.

"You can even create false tears, but all you want is power and that's all you will ever want!" He shouted with violence in his eyes. I grabbed him and pushed him up against the wall.

"No! Abel, please listen to me! I once felt that way, but not anymore! I do care about you and I do love you! Please Abel, listen to me!" I implored. I had him pinned along the wall and he called for his guards. I stared at him, then kissed his lips and whispered, "I love you, my brother."

At first I felt him squirm, then I felt him melt against me. I heard now the guards coming into the room. I was pulled away from him with my eyes closed. I opened them and yelled out his name, "Abel!"

He was frozen there, shocked and in silence. I was dragged out of the castle and thrown out of the gates. I was covered in mud and my horse, Mage, was still within the castle. I was miserable and I could feel the rain covering my face. I looked up and spied the window that my brother was looking out of. I saw his face in the window staring down at me. I sighed and got up. I yelled at the guards to bring me my horse as I heard Mage neigh within the gates. One guard opened the gate and lead Mage out. I jumped up on my horse and rode off, and then turned back to look at the window before leaving completely and noticed Abel was still there, watching me.

"I do love you, my brother," I whispered, but I knew he could not hear me and it only hurt me to say it. I continued to ride through the day, soaked from the rain. My face was covered in mud and I thought of Sir Leo. I wondered if he could possibly understand me.

As the hours passed, the rain stopped and the sun returned. There was a small pond in the woods where I stopped to wash off the mud on my face. I looked at myself in the reflection and saw my hair covering my eyes and still soaked from the rain. The ribbon that had kept my hair neatly tied had fallen low and had practically fallen off. My eyes were bluer than the water.

I whispered to myself, “I am a monster disguised as an angel…” I did not want to go home. I did not want to go anywhere. I wanted to stay soaked in my misery and suffer for my thoughts I once had for my brother. *I deserve this along with anything else that comes to me for my dreams of power and greed, control and suffering. Who am I to have these things? What do they really mean to me?* I thought dejectedly. The love of my brother was enough to lead me to question everything I knew before. How could I have been so wrong?

I was exhausted, but I could not stop thinking of him. *This,* I decided, *was where I must decide which is better: love or power? Which one will I be most happy with? It's just like the old woman said.* I was staring at the water when I heard the sound of a flute appear out of nowhere. Where was this sound coming from? All of a sudden, a bright glow appeared, blinding me. It was so intense that I covered my eyes with my arm and fell over onto the ground. When I thought the vivid glow had disappeared, I removed my arm from my eyes and saw a woman covered in a transparent white robe that floated weightlessly around her. What was this?

Her face was covered with the same sheer fabric so that I could barely see her eyes, nose, and mouth. I wanted to touch the material and see who this woman was when suddenly; I heard her voice surround me. She spoke with words that filled both my ears as if she was right next to me.

"Welcome, Prince Kain," she said gently. I wondered what I was welcomed to. She simply floated above the ground and glowed with a light that was brighter than my brother's.

"I am the Goddess of peace and love," She continued as I stared at her.

"The Goddess of peace and love? What are you doing talking to me?" I asked in bewilderment.

"That is it, Prince Kain. I was told by the God of light to speak with you and warn you of what lies ahead." She replied.

"The God of Light sent you? Why? Why would the God of light care about me?" I responded angrily… but why was I angry?

She then sighed with her white hair floating in the air. "Even though you were chosen by the God of darkness, it does not mean the God of light does not love you," she assured me, "He cares deeply about you and does not wish for you to fall into the hands of Sceptor. The God of light, Vertigo, desires for you to follow his command."

She began to fade away along with the light until I could see the forest behind her. "Wait! Do not go, not yet! Please!" I implored.

She spoke once more, "Do not forget my words and do not complete false destinies, Prince Kain….Kain….ain…" Her voice echoed through the forest, growing ever fainter. I did not know what to do. Why would the Goddess of peace and love come to lead me toward the God of light? *This Vertigo... How can I believe her or even trust her? What if they wish my death? My Gods, what do I do?*

I rested in the sunshine next to the pond and began to get quite hungry. My clothes were practically dry, as well as my hair. I thought perhaps now I could ride into a small village and grab a bite to eat. I got up and saw Mage grazing several yards away. My mind had almost forgotten of my brother after that woman spoke with me, which was good in a way because I was becoming quite depressed from the memory of it. At that point, I felt nearly restored to my old self.

I jumped on Mage and I knew he was irritated with me; I was asking him to ride when he was busy eating. I laughed a bit and said, "Come on boy, you can eat when we get to a tavern." He made a muffled whine, but began riding as I asked him to.

I traveled past hills and valleys, over rivers, and through mountains. I began to notice the same old village I ran into last time when I was going to see my brother. I hated this village for everyone here knew me and inexplicably disliked me. I jumped off my horse and walked into the tavern. The same man approached me from last time and asked me if I wanted something to eat or drink.

"I would like some wine along with whatever type of meat or bread you have," I ordered. The man nodded and went into the back room. I looked around from my table and saw that everyone was staring at me again. I ignored them for I was too hungry to leave or start a fight. It was not long before my food arrived. The man brought me meaty pieces of chicken along with a small loaf of warm bread and a cup of wine. All of it was hearty and delicious; I had to give him credit for that. When I finished, I left some money on the table and a bit of a tip for the enchanting meal. Mage was resting when I came out of the tavern and I hopped up on his back. Many of the villagers outside were watching me as I ordered Mage to ride like the wind.

Chapter Four
Message of a Knight

When I got back, it was extremely late and all I wanted to do was sleep. I walked in dirty, tired and afraid of what Ariaus was going to say to me. Why was I afraid? I felt that I was supposed to hate my brother; Ariaus wanted me to, but why? I walked into the most spacious chamber in the castle to see if Ariaus was there and he was, as usual. I went up to the large armchair near the fireplace and kneeled down in front of him with my eyes half open. I could not see him, for the shadow covered his face again and I could care less if he was angry at me or not. I was tired, so I laid my head down on his leg and closed my eyes. He did not say anything, but I felt a hand reach for my head and begin sliding its fingers through my hair. Ariaus was picking out twigs that had stuck in there throughout the day.

"You are a mess, boy. What have you done to yourself?" He inquired with his lips curling in distaste. I said nothing and continued to rest on his lap. I did not want to move, for I was finding myself beginning to fall asleep. Ariaus knew I was tired; I felt him move me. To my surprise, he picked me up and carried me upstairs.

How the hell does this man do that? I thought groggily. Ariaus must be very strong for his age to be able to carry me in his arms. He laid me down on my bed, taking off my muddy, dry boots and sliding off my coat. He untied my vest as well as my black puffy shirt. I tried hard not to smile because I wanted him to think I was sleeping; I could feel him looking at me. He untied the loose ribbon on my hair and began stroking my head again. I could smell his cologne that he wore. Then, before I knew it, I felt his warm lips touching my cheek. He also had long fingernails like my brother and

I. I still pretended to be asleep. In spite of my pretense, I do believe he knew I was awake. With my eyes still closed, I could feel him rise from his seat. He stared at me again for an entire ten minutes before quietly leaving the room. Why did I pretend to be asleep? I should have awoken! I opened my eyes, smiled, and then turned over to sleep.

That night, I dreamed of my brother. He was crying next to the window. I dreamed I was a ghost and could not touch him or hold him. All I could do was watch him in pain. It was not truly a dream for the fear and anxiety struck within me; it was a nightmare. I hated it and I wanted to wake up immediately, but I could not rouse myself. I felt like I was falling and I could not stop. I was lost in my own shame. All I could say to myself was, "I love you Abel, I am sorry…I am so… very… sorry…"

When I awoke, I felt alone and the sun was not shining in the room. The Gods only knew what time it was when I had awoken that morning. I went to the window and opened the curtains to let the sun shine in. I wanted my castle to be bright and beautiful, like my brother's, but I could not stand the brightness, so I left the room. I went back inside when my eyes had adjusted to the light.

I grabbed a silk robe and went downstairs to order a few of my servants to draw me a bath. I could not wait to bathe, for I was filthy and could not stand it any longer. I did not see Ariaus anywhere and I wondered where he might be. My servants began drawing me a bath and I urged for them to finish it quickly. When they were finished, I lit a few candles and incense to help me relax. There was a small window in the bathing room, so I moved to open it to let some light in the room. Now, all I wished for was some fresh flowers, but did I even have a garden to allow fresh flowers to grow? No!

I sighed and took off my old clothes from last night. I began climbing into the bathtub, which was surrounded by candles of different sizes. I relaxed in the warmth of the water and I could hear the birds outside singing. The sound was beautiful and it relieved the tension and stress from my journey. I could have fallen asleep in there, but I probably would have drowned. I did not want to leave this small pool of warmth and relaxation. Covered in bubbles, I went under the water to wash my hair. Leaves and sticks began coming out and floated to the surface. It was a damn bird's nest, I tell you! I could have hatched thirteen chicks in my hair at once. I swished it around and scrubbed it with soap and sweet-smelling oils. It felt good and I could not wait to see Ariaus all cleaned up and in clean clothes. I rinsed my hair and rose out of the tub. I grabbed my robe and a piece of cloth to dry myself with.

Slipping on my robe, I went out of the room and into the main hall of the castle. I turned towards the stairs and when I looked up, I saw Ariaus staring down at me. He had a small smile on his face, and the window beside him threw light out upon him. He looked like some dark angel standing there on the red carpeted steps.

"Good morning, master." I said to him kindly with a soft smile back to him. He slowly walked down the steps and kissed my cheek.

"How was your sleep, Kain?" He asked pleasantly.

I told him that it was nice, even though I had a terrible nightmare of my brother. He stood there, trying to read my thoughts, but I did not allow him to. I blocked my thoughts and whispered, "I wish to go to my room and change into some clean clothes, if you do not mind."

He smiled and said, "Of course I do not mind, dear boy." He moved out of my way so that I may walk up the stairs. He had a very slow and graceful stride. I ran up the stairs to my bedchamber and shut the door. I pulled out a white puffy shirt and put it on me. I then pulled out a pair of black pants and a black velvet vest that I adored before admiring myself in the mirror. I looked elegant in my clothes; I could have kissed myself. I slid on my black leather boots to top off the ensemble. Grabbing my brush, I began to brush out my hair that had almost completely dried. I took a black lace ribbon from my desk and tied my hair back with it very gently. Like my brother, I allowed pieces of my bangs to fall in front of my eyes. I smiled in the mirror, spraying on the fragrance that Ariaus favored. I ran downstairs to see him and it seemed he was still at the bottom, as if he waited for me the entire time. I ran down there next to him and I smiled at him.

"That was quick, Kain…" He said to me with complete kindness. "It seems you are in a rush to go somewhere, dear boy."

I smiled at him and hugged him, whispering in his ear very softly, "No master, I just could not wait to see you." I felt his arm slide around my body and pull me closer to him. I could feel a smile on his face without even seeing it. I kissed his cheek. I wanted to hold him all day. I then moved back a bit to see his face and there was a grin, just as I thought. At that moment, a servant walked into the room. My master heard him and we both quickly let go of each other. The servant pretended not to see anything, then spoke.

"Master Ariaus, there is a man at the door."

Ariaus looked at me and told me to stay here. I did as he wished and began filing my nails to waste time. When he had returned, he told me it was one of the knights from my brother's castle. I was thinking which knight it could have been when Ariaus interrupted my thoughts.

"His name is Sir Leo and he said he wishes to speak with you, Kain." He declared calmly. I raised my head and stopped filing my nails.

"Did you say Sir Leo?" I inquired; baffled that he would journey such a great distance to see me. I wondered what he had wanted from me and I could not wait to see him. I had forgotten all about him and his attractive appearance. I ran to the door and reopened it. There stood the handsome man with a letter in his hand. He looked at me with his bright green eyes and soothing, yet gallant face.

"Sir Leo!" I exclaimed with surprise, "What is it you wish of me?"

He looked at me and handed me a letter. "I've ridden far to hand this to you. I figured it is important for you to have this now, knowing what happened between you and Abel. It was specifically written for you," he mentioned as he pointed at the envelope with his index finger. "See? The seal is still unbroken. This is from your father that passed away five years ago. He knew you would not return to the castle before his death. Your father was very ill for a great deal of time," he announced in a solemn tone.

I looked at the letter and then back to Leo. He stood there looking dejected and innocent, his raven black hair falling in front of his eyes. I thought about my father, which was something I had barely done before that moment. I did not dare open the letter now for I knew I was going to cry if I did. I looked up at Leo again.

"Would you like to come in, Sir Leo? I would not mind at all if you wish to do so, perhaps for some tea?" I invited him with a welcoming gesture. I stared at him, hoping he would say yes. When he nodded at the generous thought, I allowed him to walk in. I looked at Ariaus that I had forgotten was there and he did not look at all pleased about this idea. I walked Leo over to the table and arranged for my servants to brew us some tea. He sat there staring at me and I fought the desire to kiss his cheek. He was dressed in his usual black leather clothing and his sword by his side.

"How is my brother?" I asked him with concern.

"He is not speaking to anyone, my prince," he replied with a troubled expression. "He has been in his room since you left. If he were to let anyone know how he is, it would have been me, but not even I have been able to get through to him. What I do know is that you were thrown out of the castle. Why is that, if I may ask?" I looked down and wondered who told Leo to bring me this letter if he has not spoken to my brother.

"Not to change the subject charming one, but if you have not spoken to my brother, then who told you to deliver this letter to me and how did you know where I lived?" I inquired.

"Why, I was told to take it to you by an elderly woman wearing a hooded cloak that came to the door last night. She said he was a friend of your father's. She even told me where to find you," he said softly. I stared at his eyes for he was drawing me into him again. I shook my head and looked down.

"I see…well, the reason why I was thrown out is because I wished to leave my brother that day," I explained. "He was expecting me to stay for longer and grew angry with me. He thought I did not love him and he was beginning to think of the stories that the elders told him about me…" I stopped talking for I thought of what I was just about to say. I looked away and tried to change the subject.

"It does not matter, for I love my brother," I declared.

"I know of these tales, my prince. They have been told by many," he informed me. I looked directly at him with my eyes wide, practically glowing in their blue-white color.

"You know of the stories… of my destiny? How I was chosen by the dark God?" I asked more shocked than before.

He nodded and whispered, "Yes my prince, but like your brother, I have not taken these fabrications to heart."

I looked down and began to recall how everyone was looking at me in the tavern. It was all coming back to me; they stared at me because they knew of these stories. They knew who I was and knew about how I was chosen by Sceptor.

"My Gods! That is why everyone has treated me strangely. Sir Leo…" I remarked and touched his shoulders, moving closer to him, staring into his eyes. "You must tell my brother that I love him, and let him know that I need help on what to do next. Please Sir Leo, will you do this for me?"

He nodded and smiled at me. "For you my prince, I would do anything!" he exclaimed. His smile became brighter and I beamed back at him. I noticed myself pushing him closer to me and kissing his cheek.

I whispered against his ear, "Thank you…"

He then kissed my cheek and whispered on mine, "You are most welcome, my prince…"

My Gods, I do believe I melted in his arms. I moved away from him slowly and sat back down in my seat. I sipped my tea while watching him with a smile. He was smiling at me while a rosy pink spread across my cheeks. Was I as flustered as he was? I must have been for I kept looking down with a grin. He was incredibly handsome! Did he notice how attractive he was or was he blind to seeing himself in the mirror?

He stood up and whispered, "Well, I must get going my prince, for I have a long journey ahead of me. I've been gone from prince Abel too long." I stood up with him, still holding the tea in my hand.

"So soon, Sir Leo? I do wish you could stay longer." I said while smiling at him, sounding identical to my brother from the other night.

"I do as well, but it is best I go, for it is my job to protect your brother," he replied. I nodded at him and understood. I wished so much he could stay with me. Again, I had forgotten that Ariaus was in a dark corner and watching the two of us the entire time. I looked at him for a minute and then walked Leo up to the door.

"Thank you for bringing me this letter, Sir Leo," I remarked.

"You're welcome. By the way, the tea was delicious," he replied while turning to face me. He winked charmingly at me and then walked out the door. I watched him, still holding my cup of tea as he leapt up on his white horse. I heard him shout out as he rode off, "Good day, my prince!"

His horse galloped off into the dark forest. I smiled and then felt a hand touch my shoulder. Turning, I saw Ariaus and looked away from him, walking over to the table were Leo's tea was. I put mine down next to his and beckoned the servants to take them away. I sat down, looking at the letter and feeling a bit of jealousy from Ariaus. I ignored him. The more I ignored him the more I felt the envy within him swell. He approached me and snatched the letter right from my hands. I shot a glare up at him in shock.

"Master! That was written by my father! Please give it back!" I begged.

He looked down at me and tore the letter into pieces before my eyes. I stood up and a tear trickled down my face.

"NO! What are you doing! Return it to me!" I grabbed the shredded paper from his hands and at the next moment, I felt a powerful slap across my face. I looked at him with complete hate and anger. My eyes darkened and my teeth were exposed between my parted lips. I pushed him out of my way and ran outside, immediately prepared my horse, grabbed the reins, and jumped upon his back. Riding like the wind, I set off to see if I could catch up to Leo. I saw the tracks of his horse and sensed that I was close. When I arrived at the darkest part of the forest, I spied Leo surrounded by wolves.

Wolves out at this time of the day? I wondered, baffled at the sight. I unsheathed my sword and rode past one of the beasts that growled and trapped Leo against a tree. Swinging my sword, I cut its mangy head off. Then, I went after another one that tried to attack Mage. My steed, nervous from his surroundings, was jumping up and down and making it difficult for me to kill the wolves that were attacking the knight. I then saw him run up to one of the creatures and slide his sword straight into it.

"Get back, Leo!" I shouted. I swung my sword to the left and sliced it right through the back of one of the ferocious beasts. Then, another felt the steel of my weapon slice through its body. Before I knew it, the rest grew frightened and took off into the forest. I jumped off my horse and noticed there was a gash on Leo's arm, a large bite mark from one of the wolves' teeth. I got on my knees and pulled Leo down with me.

"You're hurt badly…we must wrap it up well so you lose no more blood," I said consolingly. He stared at me with the wolves' blood coated on my face and hands. I paid no heed and took the ribbon from my hair and tied it tightly around his arm. He watched my long black hair fall below my shoulders. He sat leaning against the tree and I felt him reach up and stroke a loose strand. I looked up at him and managed a genuine smile.

"You and your brother have such beautiful hair," He said with an innocent and boyish face that I could have kissed at any minute.

"Why thank you, Sir Leo." I could not stop grinning. I hoisted him up on his feet and noticed he was still touching my hair.

"You really like my hair, don't you?" I said to him softly. He looked at me and I gazed back at him. He moved his eyes on his horse and saw that he was covered with blood. I looked over at it as well and I placed my fingers against its neck to feel if he had a pulse. I gulped, as I did not feel any blood pumping. We both knew at that moment that he was dead. Leo bent to one knee and closed his eyes.

"May the Gods and Goddesses of light protect him on his journey," said he. Leo rose up slowly and continued, "He was a faithful horse, and wonderful to be around. He was a dear friend to me." I stared at him and watched him drown in his sadness. What would I have done if that was Mage? I walked slowly over to him and kissed him softly on his cheek.

"I am sorry Leo," I whispered softly into his ear. I felt him turn and wrap his arms around me and rest his head on my shoulder. I held him close to me and felt him pull me closer. Why did I love this affection so much? I held him until he moved away from me slowly.

"Why did you ride after me?" He inquired. He turned to face me and I stared back at him. I do not understand why I actually rode after him. I had a feeling inside that made me do it.

"This might seem strange, but I do not know why, Sir Leo," I replied, still wondering.

He looked at me strangely and said, "If you did not ride after me, I would have died by the wolves. My Prince, you saved my life." He stared at me, and then said gently, "Thank you." He got down on one knee and kissed my hand like he did when I first met him. "I owe you my life now. If I can do anything for you, I will," he whispered with my hand in his. He closed his eyes, kissing my hand again. *Oh my Gods please do not stop*! I thought with a shiver. I smiled down at him and watched him stand up to face me eye-to-eye.

"How am I to return to the castle?" he asked, softly staring at me. I knew it was I who was going to have to take him back, but I had no problem with it. I smiled charmingly at him, showing my teeth.

"Of course beautiful one, I will take you," I said. He beamed and laughed heartily.

"I love how you call me beautiful one when you should take a damn good look in the mirror," he said slyly. He walked over to my horse and patted him, which made me visibly blush. I jumped up on my horse and Leo leapt behind me. He wrapped his arms around me to hold on through the ride and held me through the entire time. I did not want him to let me go. I took a more scenic path this time to make the trip longer so that I could spend the night with him. Admittedly, even if I took the shorter path, I would have needed to still spend the night with him. Along the way, I could feel him fall asleep on my shoulder. We were riding for hours, but I could have ridden for another twelve or more. Finally, I stopped the horse as we reached a wide lake.

"Leo? Wake up," I whispered as he awakened. His eyes were half-lidded quite adorably and I wanted to kiss him. "We have to spend the night," I continued. "We will continue our ride tomorrow morning."

He nodded, still tired, and he walked over to a soft spot on the ground. I pulled out two blankets that I kept in a bag that was tied to my horse. Mage trotted over to a patch of tall grass to graze as he usually does when we stop after a ride. I laid out one blanket to sleep on, and then laid down on it, using my coat as a pillow, as he did the same. I pulled a second blanket over us and he came closer to me. My hair was all over the place and right before I moved to get it out of the way, Leo did it for me. I stared at him lying down and smiling sweetly at me. He continued to move my hair out of the way so that it was above my head. He rolled over on his back as I felt a shiver.

"It's dreadfully cold out here," I exclaimed. I was on my side facing him and he instructed for me to turn around. I did as he wished, turning to face Mage. My eyes widened as I felt his arm wrap around me from behind. My body warmed, I closed my eyes with a smile.

"Goodnight, Leo..." I whispered.

"Goodnight my prince," Leo whispered in my ear the moment before I drifted off to sleep.

Chapter Five
Adventure Awaits

The next morning, I awoke with Leo by my side. I slept close to him the entire night to keep warm. He held me until the sun roused us. He rubbed his eyes like a little boy while I tied back my hair with a handkerchief that I had kept it in my pocket for some time. Watching with affection as Leo slowly rose from the covers, I walked over to Mage and patted his head. I began to yawn and stretch when I heard Leo's voice.

"Kain? Did you sleep well?" He inquired in a groggy tone. I smiled when he spoke and walked over to him.

"Indeed I did, my friend," I said while kissing his cheek. "We must get going now. There is a village up ahead were we can get some food."

He smiled at me and watched me leap up on my horse. He followed along behind me, wrapping his arms around me again. We followed the pathway that led us to a two-way fork in the road. There was a sign in the middle that swung back and forth. To make matters worse, it also twirled in the breeze, revealing an arrow pointing both east and west, depending on the wind's direction. I wanted to go west, but it was hard to tell which direction it was, for the sign did not stop spinning around in circles. I turned my head to look at Leo.

"Great, what do we do?" I said to him. He pointed to the east when I thought we should have headed west.

"I do believe we should travel on the east path; it looks safer," Leo said cautiously. He was right about that, although they both appeared to be safe roadways.

"My friend, let's head east and we can see what happens and where it leads us. Is that all right with you?" I inquired, prepared to compromise. He nodded at my request and took to the east. I felt him hold me tighter, as if he was afraid of something. The pathway became darker as we rode deeper into the forest.

"What was that!?" Leo exclaimed, startled. "Did you hear that, my prince?"

"I didn't hear anything. There is nothing there. Now calm down my friend," I replied soothingly. I nudged Mage to continue riding and he did as I commanded. I then began to hear something as well. It made a scratchy sound and I stopped Mage to see if I could spot what was causing it.

"I heard something too, Leo," I told him quietly.

He held me tighter, to the point where I could barely breathe. I squinted my eyes to try to make out what was the cause of the noise.

"Leo, that's too tight." I squeaked.

"I am sorry, My Prince," he replied.

I peered around the forest to gauge if I could see anything, when right at the corner of my eye, I saw a creature! It was a small and ugly beast that moved swiftly. The creature popped up in front of Mage, causing him to buck.

"No, Mage! Down!" I tried to calm him before he knocked Leo and I off his back, making us fall hard on our backs on the earth below us. I saw Leo pull out his sword as I did the same.

"Back, demon! Back!" I shouted. The creature slowed enough at last for me to make out what it was; it was a stout goblin-man with a bushy beard and beady, monstrous crimson eyes. His beastly features and limbs were comparable to that of a human, yet warped and hairy like that of an animal.

"Go back to where you came from, humans. You have no place here!" it said with an ugly sneer on its face. "This is my land!" it growled.

"Who are you to tell us we have no place here! Now move out of my way, monster! Do you know who I am? I am the Prince of Tarot and brother to Prince Abel!" I exclaimed, waving my sword in the air. Leo stood and continued to point his sword at the creature. The hobgoblin moved from our way cautiously, with a frown upon his snarly face.

"Prince Kain, we all know of you and your cruel hearted ways! It is not I who is the monster! It is you!" It grumbled at us. "There is a witch in that direction; she'll eat your heart out, if you even have one!" It cackled to itself, with drool dripping down its filthy, moist chin.

"How *putrid*," I muttered to myself. I did not listen to the foul creature, for I had to bring Leo back home before it grew dark again. We continued to ride down the dirt-laden path and all the while, the way grew murkier and more frightening, although thankfully, slowly more and more devoid of the goblin's stench. My body tensed with excitement; I was prepared for any battle and I do love to clash swords with a worthy adversary. There was fog lining the path that grew thicker with every step. It was hard to see where I was going. Leo was quiet and I did not know why. I tried to speak to him with little avail.

"Are you feeling well, my friend?" I inquired with care.

"Yes my prince," he responded in a soft tone, his arms still tightly wound around my waist. He spoke so sweetly that I could have melted. I beamed and continued to ride Mage through the dark, misty pathway. After an hour passed, I began to see through the fog more clearly than before. At last, I came to a clearing that revealed a small cobblestone house with tiny windows. There were large vines covering the structure as if they were devouring it. I jumped off Mage and halted as I heard a warning from Leo.

"No! How do you know it's safe?" He asked, startled. I looked at him and smiled.

"We will never know until we take a look, now will we?" I replied with a wink. I grinned at him and he shook his head. He jumped off the horse first and pulled out his sword. I waved for him to put his sword back, for those that lived here would think we were after them. I went up to the decrepit wooden door of the cottage and knocked softly. I stood there and waited for several minutes.

"It seems no one is home. Let's continue onward, then," Leo remarked.

"Leo, we need something to eat and we must know how to get off this pathway or to where it takes us," I insisted.

"Perhaps we should simply turn around and take the opposite path back at the fork in the road," Leo reasoned. I laughed at his response.

"That will take us ages, while this pathway must eventually lead out of the forest," I replied. I turned away from the door, but as soon as I began to walk away, I heard a voice behind me.

"Welcome, dear boy; I have been expecting you," said a creaky voice from within the shadow of the doorway. I knew that voice! I turned around and there I saw the same old woman I met several days ago in the forest before I went to see my brother.

"You? What are you doing here, old woman?" I asked in bewilderment. I heard her annoying cackle and all I wanted to do was cover my ears. "You're looking very..." I tilted my nose upward and sniffed, "*Unwashed* this evening." She burst out into a hysterical fit of chuckles, causing her to hack and cough unsightly phlegm. After several minutes of watching her and figuring she was going to croak before my eyes, she responded.

"You always know how to flatter a lady," she said with a ghastly smile.

"Do you know this woman?" Leo said suspiciously.

"Sadly, I do." I responded with a wrinkled nose. She began laughing again.

"Come now, step inside for something to eat and drink. I know that is what you wish for, No?" She said with a raspy chuckle. I looked at Leo as he just looked down.

"Well, we could both use some food and drink. Come on Leo, it is safe here," I stated. I wrapped my arm around his shoulder and led him into the old woman's house.

The interior of the old hut was dark and dusty, but I could smell the pleasant scent of homemade bread and fresh coffee. The old woman had a raven for a pet that flew over to my shoulder as soon as I sat down. Leo watched the raven and laughed to himself. I smiled at him and again at the sociable bird.

"Well well, I see you met my friend Gordock," She laughed again as she spoke. She served us some bread and poured fresh coffee into black teacups with rims painted in beautiful white details that appeared to be decorated by hand.

"I do believe I like this old woman," Leo grinned and whispered in my ear. "She seems a bit familiar, but I can't place it in my mind from whence I met her."

"She is not all that bad, I guess," I whispered back and smiled. I took a hearty bite of the fresh bread and gave a small piece of it to the black raven. The bird then flew over to the old woman and began happily eating his piece. She then sat down at the table with us and watched us eat.

"So old woman, do tell us how to get out of here, so I may reach my brother's palace," I requested. She looked at Leo, then back at me, and smiled.

"You cannot go there just yet, dear boy. You have a long journey ahead of you. Ariaus found out that you broke the link of power he used to control you. You see, Ariaus works for the Dark God and he was going to use you to help summon Sceptor into the world."

"What do you mean I broke the link?" I gasped with my eyes wide with shock. She took my hand and looked straight into my eyes.

"Dear boy, you found out that the entire meaning to life is not power and destruction, but instead, love. Now, you still hold the gift of power from the Dark God, but you must learn how to use it. There is a man on Mount Canovas that can teach you everything you need to know about your powers. From there, seek out the lost sword, Nebula. After he teaches you the magic, you must ask him about a tower not far from his location and how to reach it. Within this tower is a key. There, it will guide you to a map. That is your ticket to the sword. It is the weapon that Ariaus wanted you to obtain. You must get to it before Ariaus does, for he will use it to destroy you and your brother," She warned.

"Head to the mountain as swiftly as possible, for Ariaus is now on a hunt for you," She explained gravely. "It is for the best that you got lost in this forest, for it helps slow him down from catching you. Once he finds you, he will force you to use your powers for evil and make you destroy your brother. Abel is the only man alive that holds the power from the God of Light. You must protect him from Ariaus and you must find the man on Mount Canovas. You have a long journey ahead of you and I wish you luck. I do hope that you succeed, handsome young man. Leo will help you on this journey,"

"I will?" Leo asked, turning his head to me in bewilderment. His face then shifted into a courageous expression. "I will!" He exclaimed. The old woman then smiled and looked at me, then Leo. Leo then turned to me, then back at her.

"I guess I could, but how do we tell Prince Abel were I am and warn him of Ariaus' intensions?" I asked. The old woman closed her eyes and then reopened them.

"Do not worry about that, dear boy. I will take care of swiftly delivering the message to him. As you know Kain, Ariaus is a powerful being. Do be careful, both of you," She warned. The old woman rose from her seat and walked over to a green velvet box. She came back to the table and handed me a large purple amulet attached to an elegant golden chain. I took it in my hand and gazed at it.

"I remember seeing this same stone around my brother's neck," I remarked.

The old woman smiled at me and whispered, "Yes, it is the stone of power. It will help you become stronger in using your abilities." I placed the stone around my neck. To my amazement, it began to glow before dying back to its original dullness. The black raven flew over to Leo's shoulder then to mine. "Perhaps I should let my little friend Gordock come along with you to help guide you through your journeys," she said with a grin. I looked at the old woman.

"You would not mind that at all?" I asked her charmingly.

"Of course not dear boy, plus I see that Gordock would in fact quite enjoy it," she chuckled. In response, the raven made squawking noises with its beak and the crone started to laugh. Leo and I joined in soon after.

The woman wished us well while Leo and I walked out the door. I jumped up on my horse along with Leo behind me and we set off to Mount Canovas. We rode down the path past the old hag's decrepit house and through the muddy path beyond. Eventually, we came to a large pond surrounded by fireflies, enjoyed the beauty of the flickering lights, and rode ever farther. Leo scanned around while I had Mage trudge through thick mud and over rugged stone. After many hours of riding, we finally came to a large open plain beyond the woods where the mountains could be seen in the distance.

"That Dark Mountain is where the old woman said we had to go," remarked Leo.

I nodded to what Leo said and began riding Mage more quickly over the flat, tall grassland. The sun shined down on our faces and I knew then that the day was then more than halfway over. I continued to ride Mage for another hour until we at last approached the base of the towering mountain and spied a trail that would take us safely over it. I nudged Mage to set forth when I heard very large birds circling around us from above. Gordock shifted about uneasily on my shoulder; he was unsettled by the feeling of this place.

Along the way, I spied the bones of animals. As we went around the large mountain, the trail led us higher and higher. Leo turned his head to face the mountain, for he did not enjoy looking down. I laughed softly to myself and continued the long ride toward the top. When we finally arrived at the summit, I spied a hulking tower built of gleaming ebony stone. Its roof was pointed as if to blend with the shape of the mountaintop.

"This has to be it, my prince," remarked Leo with a satisfied tone. I nodded to him and dismounted from my horse. Gordock was still perched on my shoulder and Leo followed behind me with his hand on his sword, ready to draw it any moment. I walked up to the large wooden door, painted black to match the ebony stone around it. It was massive enough to fit a dragon through it. The door opened without me even knocking. I walked in and spied two people on either side wearing black robes and hoods standing to hold the doors.

"I don't like the look of this place." Leo whispered in my ear as he grabbed my arm.

"Do not worry, Leo," I responded softly.

The doors shut behind us as the two robed beings passed by to escort us through the tower. They led us to a large room where a fireplace and three armchairs were. The interior was dark and it was hard to see far ahead. It reminded me of Ariaus' Castle. I walked up to one of the chairs and sat down in one. Leo followed me while Gordock still perched on my shoulder. The two robed beings walked over to another large set of doors to the side of the fireplace and opened them slowly, revealing a grand marble staircase.

Once the doors were opened, a tall figure wearing a red velvet robe and hood walked down the stairs and into the chamber alongside the two cloaked footmen. I could not see any of their faces. I could feel Leo's hand touch my arm. I touched his hand and held it while the being walked slowly closer to us. I watched it carcfully as thc othcr two black robcd bcings shut thc door behind the one in red. They stood by the entrance and bowed their heads. The one in red velvet walked gracefully over to the third armchair.

"Welcome, dark prince, to the summit of Mount Canovas ," The being said in a deep tone of voice. When he spoke, it caused a rumble in my heart and I felt Leo's hand grip me harder.

I raised an eyebrow and thought, *dark prince? What does that mean?* The deep voiced being began to laugh and the sound echoed throughout the tower walls. I closed my eyes tightly when he roared, for it was very loud. It seemed he was not human for having such a powerful voice.

"Why, you are the dark prince. You are the chosen one, aren't you?" He spoke again, shaking my heart and hurting my ears.

"Yes, I am the chosen one and I came to learn how to use my power. It was given to me by the God Sceptor," I said to him with a bit of a shaky voice. Leo just sat there, staring and clutching my hand.

"I see, and you wish me to teach you these powers, am I correct?" He remarked, his face still obscured by his hood.

"Yes…" I said, nodding at the same time, a piece of my hair falling in front of my eyes again. I looked up at it and tried to blow it away with my breath, but it did not work. I felt myself getting very nervous and afraid of what was going to happen. The figure stood up from his seat and extended his hand out to me. His fingers were white, paler than my own skin. His nails were longer than anyone's I have ever seen. His long sleeve hung loosely to his knuckles. I reached out to take his hand. It was cold and it made me want to let go of him as I felt a shiver deep in my spine.

"Come with me, I will teach you what you need to know," He said, amused. I stood up, mesmerized by him and trying to see his appearance. I was lost in him and had nearly forgotten of Leo. I was taken to the doors that he came from. I faintly heard Leo in the back yell out my name. He was being held down by the two beings in the black robes. Gordock flew toward the struggle, but was snatched by one of the hooded figures. I wanted to run to them, but I could not move on my own accord. All I could do was walk forward to where the red-robed being took me.

We reached an enormous wooden door, which he opened by himself with extraordinary force. I could not believe the sight. I walked through the doors into a dark room where there was a circle drawn in the middle of the marble floored room. The circle had strange symbols on it and glowed in purple. All I could do was watch this as he shut the doors behind us. In the obscurity of the room, all I saw was the circle. Pitch blackness and darkness surrounded me. It was very strange to see this and I did not know what would happen next. I was lost in this amazing place. I could not even see where the being in red was. I then felt a hand touch my shoulder and I turned around to see if it was him, which it was, and he led me to the center of the circle.

"Now I want you to concentrate on what I do," He said gravely. I listened completely to what he said and watched his every move. He pulled his hood away from his head and I saw his very long, black hair. It was straight and his face was white like his hands were. His eyes were purple, the same hue as the glowing circle beneath us. I saw how his face was shaped, long and thin. His eyebrows were black and thick. His lips were dark purple. His robe had become a much darker color, its shade dimmed by the brilliance of the bright purple glow shining up from below us. I watched him as he aimed a sly grin at me. He then raised his arms to the side and whispered some type of cabalistic words. It was not in any language I knew and it frightened me. The circle grew brighter and now lit up the entire room.

My Gods! Was this a trap? Will I die here or did I do the right thing? I thought in a panic. I then felt something large breathing down my neck and when I turned around, there was an enormous black dragon! He was covered in the same purple light as the circle below. I screamed and fell to the ground until I felt a large hand lift me back on my feet. I was terribly frightened and I felt myself begin to cry.

The dragon was directly in my face and roared with a terrible sound. I covered my ears and screamed, tears coming down my eyes. The man in his red robe was cackling eagerly. I looked up at him and I saw laughter in his eyes. I began hitting him and pulling out my sword to attack him with it. With a grin, he grabbed my arm and threw me down to the ground. I looked behind me to see if the terrifying sight was there, but it was gone. I sat on the ground staring up at the man with the long black hair. What did he have in mind for me? Did he find frightening me fun? I then heard his loud, powerful voice.

"Dark Prince, why do you try to hurt the one who teaches you?" he said while laughing at the same time.

"Teach me!? You dare not teach me, but instead try to frighten me! Just what is it you wish to do with me here in this monstrous room!?" I demanded.

He then began laughing again and I heard him say, "I am only showing you how great your power is. You can conjure many spirits, just like the one I showed you. That dragon was a demonstration on how you can use your inner power to call upon life forces and create monsters from your mind." I looked at him, my eyebrows covering my eyes to make them look dark and hidden. I stood up to face him.

"All right then, enough demonstrations. Teach me how to do these things," I demanded. He grinned and bowed.

"Why of course. For you to start, let us create fire in the palm of your hand. To do this, you must see it strongly in your mind, then feel it manifest. Do you see now?" He declared with confidence.

I held out my hand and tried to see the flame there before trying to create it as he instructed. I did not see anything happen, but then I felt his hand touch mine.

"Dark prince, you must feel the power within you. It lies deep inside of you, in the depths of your soul. Now try again," He said.

I tried again and this time, I sought out the ability within me. As I concentrated forcefully, I sensed an incredible power welling up from inside. I felt suddenly as if I was invincible, as if I could do anything and no one could stop me. I felt my hair blow upwards. *Could it be my power causing this?* I watched the flame grow within my hand and the more I watched, the more powerful I felt. My hair was whipping around more fiercely. In that moment, I knew that if I could master this, I could do anything. The power was addictive. I could see how anyone could even let it devour their soul. I held control of it, feeding off the blissful feeling as I continued to evoke the flame within my hand.

"Nebulaaaa…" a ghostly voice echoed from the depths of the room. It thundered from the stone upon my chest as if coming from within my heart. I shook my head and looked around curiously. *What was that?* I thought as I looked at the being, but he seemed to not noticc thc haunting voicc. "Find…thc sword….Nebula." The voice appeared again and still no reaction from the being in red. I ignored it and continued on with my lesson.

"Wonderful, Kain! I knew you could do it!" The figure exclaimed as I was snapped back to reality, "By the way, I am Malus. So please, do call me by my name." I grinned at him with the flame still in my hand. I looked at my chest; my purple stone was glowing along with the bright circle on the floor. The old woman said that it would do this when my power was being used. I looked up at Malus and smiled. I knew then exactly what I needed to do.

I now knew everything that I needed to know about my abilities. Many hours had passed when I walked out of the room, although it only felt like minutes. As the massive door swung open, I shielded my eyes in pain; the dim tower had become too bright for me during the hours of training. I looked for Leo and as I approached the main room of the castle, I noticed he was tied up to his seat and motionless with Gordock tied by the talon to the head of the chair. I laughed; I couldn't help myself. I knew that he probably tried to struggle to get away, but I knew why he was restrained and it did not bother me at all.

I walked over to Leo, who had sat there with his head down, exhausted from the struggle to get loose. I had a big grin on my face when I kneeled down to him. He looked up at me and his eyes widened. I smiled at him, showing my teeth. How adorably sweet he looked when he saw me.

"Kain! Are you all right?! Did that monster hurt you!? Please answer me, my prince!" He shouted. I continued to smile at him and look at him in his eyes. How charming of him to worry if I was okay when he was the one who had to fight and get tied up to sit and be concerned. I leaned over to kiss his cheek and I began to untie him. He just sat there in silence and watched me release his bonds, then Gordock's directly afterward. I continued to grin and helped him out of the chair as the raven stretched its wings and eagerly hopped back onto my shoulder.

"Come my friend, our next thing to do is to find a lost sword called Nebula. I must gain its power and then destroy my master, Ariaus before he gets a hold of the sword and causes the world to fall to his knees," I declared.

Chapter Six
The Green-Eyed Guardian

Malus had allowed us to spend the night. Before leaving the next morning, he served us a delicious meal of all the meats we could eat and wine we could drink. It was great to fill the stomach again. I was well rested as well as Leo and we were ready to take on the next adventure. Before setting off, we discussed the path ahead.

"Malus, is there a tower nearby?" I asked, remembering the words of the old woman.

"Why yes, it is funny you ask. Beyond the mountain to the north, there is a great tower, but I warn you, beware of a large feline beast," Malus explained. "It is ferocious. I hear news often of travelers narrowly escaping the attack of this deadly creature."

It will be a long and treacherous journey, but I must do this and I will! I motivated myself. *Now, to the watch tower located north of here.* We were given enough food to bring with us on our journey as well. I attached several leather bags to Mage filled with water and food. I hugged Malus and thanked him for his help, then walked back over to Mage and jumped on his back. Leo smiled and thanked Malus, bowing to him. Leo then jumped up on Mage behind me and gave a single wave to Malus. We then started our long ride north; back down the mountain and heading forward, where another dark forest lay. I noticed the woodlands were filled with many flowers and plants and it was hard to see through the pathway. I continued to follow this road with its greenery surrounding both sides of us. I then heard Leo speak to me in my ear. I felt his warm breath when he spoke.

"My prince?" he asked me with the most charming voice.

"Yes, my friend?" I said with a smile, still looking forward and guiding Mage through the green forest.

"Do you think that old woman let Prince Abel know what we were doing, and that Ariaus is after him?" He inquired with concern. I sat in silence for a minute before answering.

"I do not know, Leo. I hope she did, though she helped us. I do believe she will keep her word," I assured him. Leo pulled out some crumbs of bread and began feeding Gordock the pieces. The hungry bird flapped his wings a bit on my shoulder and I laughed.

"What are you doing, Leo? You're making him go wild on my shoulder," I remarked with a chuckle. Leo kept feeding it and answered my question.

"What? You know birds get hungry too, my prince." He sounded like a little boy when he said that, a child at heart with a deep soothing voice. I shook my head and laughed.

We talked throughout the ride to help pass time quickly. He made me laugh with his ridiculous tales for over an hour, telling me stories of his battles and his boyhood. I could have listened for longer, but he went quiet when we came to a misty lake. The birds outside even went quiet. I made Mage trot slowly around this area to take caution; the Gods only knew what lay ahead. Again, I felt Leo hold me tightly around my waist. I knew when he was frightened; although I was sure he believed that I never could detect it. I wanted to laugh at him, but I began feeling quite frightened myself.

"Something isn't right in the air. Do you sense it?" he asked with a hint of nervousness in his voice.

"Yes, indeed I do," I responded cautiously, but I had a feeling we were on the right track. That tower was close by and so was the large black cat, I could feel it. The air grew thick and muggy as we approached the water. I moved forward to pass by the lake when I heard a growling sound. I pulled out my sword and saw the large black catlike beast laying there with a sharp piece of glass lodged in its leg. Leo gasped at the sight of the enormous cat and held me tighter. I saw him in the corner of my eye and then stared back directly at the cat. I faced my sword straight at it. I saw it was in tremendous pain. It wanted to attack us, but it was losing blood rapidly, so much that I could smell it. I stared at its eyes and felt sympathy for it. What cruel person could leave it there to suffer? I put my sword away and jumped off my horse.

"Kain, NO!" Leo screamed to no avail. He tried to grab for me, but I told him to be quiet. I walked over to the large cat and untied the handkerchief from my hair. As I crept closer, it still tried to grab at me, but gave up from lack of blood. It was growing weak and I kneeled down next to its leg. My Gods, the leg was huge! I put my hand on the shard and pulled it from the enormous creature. The beast put its jaws together and growled at me, so close that I could smell the staleness in its breath. I closed my eyes and then wrapped its leg with the handkerchief. When I was done I slowly got up from the ground and stared down at the creature.

I turned my back and walked over to Mage, who was kicking his hooves in the dirt. I could hear the heavy breathing from the large cat. I wished it well and jumped up on my horse. Leo stared at me, not believing I was still alive. He then hugged me tightly and whispered, "I thought you were going to die! Never do that again!"

I grinned at him charmingly, revealing my polished teeth. I then told Mage to continue moving and he started off into a gallop. We rode past the lake and out of the forest. There was another open field, but this time filled with fog. In the distance, we could make out the hulking silhouette of the Tower. It was an intimidating sight, rising up and disappearing into the mist. The pathway leading up to it was lined with glorious stone statues of Gods and heroes. Gordock flew over to sit on a massive sculpture of a cat in an upright-seated position.

I turned to Leo and whispered, "This must be it, my friend! Let's go!" I began to ride Mage up to the tower doors when the large black cat jumped in front of my horse. It had a grave look on its face: not angry, but still honoring its duty to guard the tower.

I heard Leo whisper in my ear, "The damn thing is back!" Then, right before my eyes, clouds of fog surrounded and covered the panther-like beast. The fog swirled around it, creating shapes as it moved. My eyebrows came together forming darkness over my eyes, but in the mists, I could swear I saw the shape of a woman's face. "What is going on?" Leo asked, shaking his head.

The fog then faded away and the black cat was gone, replaced by a woman standing before us. She was nude and was shivering in the cold. Leo could not believe the sight; he could not tear his eyes away from her. I turned to him and waved my hand in front of his eyes, then slapped him softly across his face to wake him up. I jumped off my horse and pulled out a blanket, then ran up to the woman as she stood there still as a stone, staring at me. I wrapped her tenderly in the blanket. Her hair was black like the cat's was. Her skin was pale white and her eyes were a stunningly bright green. She watched me cover her in the blanket and I began rubbing her shoulders to warm her. She was shocked about something, but I could not figure it out. Ever since I found out how to use my power, I felt that nothing can hurt me. I have not been as afraid as I used to be.

"You could have harmed me when I was vulnerable, but you did not. For that, I am grateful. Who are you, young man?" She sounded like a goddess when she spoke.

"I am Kain, brother of Prince Abel," I responded. She then stepped back from me and bowed. My eyes widened; I did not know why she did this.

"You are the chosen one by the Dark God, Sceptor!" She exclaimed. I then looked down and back at her.

"Yes indeed my dear, I am," I confirmed.

She then kissed my hand and whispered, "Please do not hurt me. I am only the guardian of this tower. I mean no harm to you, Dark Prince."

I took my hand from her and lifted her chin to face my eyes. "My dear, stop that…I mean no harm to you either. My companion and I are on a quest for the lost sword, Nebula," I explained. Leo continued to sit on the horse and did not move.

"You must have come for the golden key then, Dark Prince. No?" She inquired.

"Yes, that is what we are here for. I will open the chest that holds the map, the one that will take us to the blade," I confirmed. I walked over to Leo and dragged him off the horse. He was still in shock from what he just saw. I kissed his cheek to bring him back to life.

"Snap out of it, my friend! We came for the key and now we are here. Come on!" I insisted. I shook him gently and he then blinked and looked at me with complete innocence. How handsome he looked, with his kindness and soft voice. I smiled at him and walked back over to the dark haired woman.

"Do you know exactly where the key is located?" I asked.

She then looked up at me and whispered, "Yes, I do. I will take you straight to it." She took my hand and led Leo and I through the doors when Gordock flew from his perch to follow. She took us up many flights of stairs. It seemed like forever and ever that we climbed. At every moment, I grew dizzier and wearier. When we finally reached the top, there was a door that was rounded at the top, its unmarked wooden exterior deceivingly plain compared to the treasure that lay inside of it. She opened it and in the middle of the room, there was a small golden chest. My eyes widened as she pointed to it.

There was a hole in the roof to allow light to shine in directly upon the chest. The light reflected magnificently upon the golden surface, making the box itself look magical and dazzling. I walked over to it and opened the lid slowly. There the key lay on the purple velvet lining inside of the chest. It was beautiful, for this was no ordinary key. It was unusually large and had many small diamonds and crystals encrusted into it. The head of the key was round and elaborately decorated with golden patterns embossed into the surface.

Now that I have this, how will it guide me to the map like the old woman said? I picked it up and held it in my hand, feeling the weight of it. It was heavy and pulsed with power in my grip. My necklace then began to glow. I noticed the decorative circular piece automatically opened, revealing a beautiful hidden compass. My eyes widened with excitement. I turned around and smiled, facing Leo and the dark hared woman. I walked over to them and showed them how beautiful it was.

"Dark Prince?" the woman said.

I then looked up at her and whispered in a soft voice, “Yes, my dear?”

She was a stunning woman with a beautifully curved body and pretty eyes. Her lips were rose-red and her porcelain skin was impossibly soft.

“I would like you to know my real name. Is that all right with you?” she said just as innocent as Leo would.

I began to laugh charmingly and whispered to her in her ear. “Of course that is all right with me.” I continued to laugh, folding my arms and holding my heart as I did so. She stood there with a tiny smile on her face.

“My name is Franchesca. I was cursed to guard this tower by an old witch many years ago. I can only be human when I am close to the tower. When I leave the tower’s surroundings, I become a panther,” she said, tears welling up in her eyes.

I looked at her sadly and wished there was a way I could help her. “Well my dear, when we find the sword, then perhaps I can break your curse and you can be human once more. It just might work if you join us in our quest. What do you say? Yes or no?” I waited for her reply and I saw her smile brightly.

“What is it I have to lose? Of course I will join you on your Quest!” She exclaimed excitedly. I knew this was working out wonderfully; we had gained someone extra to help us find this sword. I had a feeling we were going to discover it before my master did. I had to, or this world is doomed by the hand of Sceptor.

We continued back down the tower and out the doors, Gordock flying swiftly to my shoulder. I looked at the compass on the key. The needle in the center was fixed to the southeast. *This must guide us toward the sword,* I figured. I jumped up on Mage and Leo did as well. Franchesca followed behind us. As we left the area, she began to change back into the large black cat. We walked past the tower and turned to head to the southeast, towards the Sea of Lost Souls.

"We're off to the Sea of Lost Souls. The compass points us in that direction," I remarked. I felt Leo hold me, but quite differently from before. I felt his head lying on my shoulder as I looked straight ahead, blinking. I held on to the reins tightly and closed my eyes. What was he thinking? I wish I could at times peel open his mind and see what he thinks.

"Leo, what's wrong?" I asked. He just sat in silence and did not answer me. "Leo?" I repeated. I then felt him kiss my clothing on my shoulder. I looked down and felt my heart skip for a minute. I continued to ride Mage along the pathway. Leo's arm slid away from me, and then lifted to stroke my hair. Why was he acting so strange? I began to wonder how my brother was. My thoughts wandered to Ariaus and how he used to be so kind to me. Why did he do that to my father's letter? Oh, my goodness, I forgot about the letter. I still had yet to put the pieces back together and read it. Leo was still touching and playing with my hair. I wonder if he ever did the same thing to my brother. Leo was strong and tough, almost cruel looking, but deep inside him was a sweet, gentle, kind-hearted young man. We reached the top of a hill and from there, I could see the sparkling ocean in the distance. I lifted Leo's head by the chin and took a deep breath.

"The ocean smells so good…" he mumbled sleepily. I smiled at what he said; I felt the same. I continued Mage down the hill and felt Leo's head hit my shoulder again. I found myself thinking about Ariaus at the same time. I remembered things he told me that made me happy, sweet words he said that made me think he cared about me. Should I have run off the way I did to him when he tore my letter? Why would

Ariaus suddenly wish to do what the old woman said he would do? I could not see my master like that and acting cruel to me, though what he did was harsh by ripping apart my letter and then slapping me.

I then sighed and Leo heard me. I felt him hold me tighter and he seemed to moan. I felt he was very sad about something and he was not telling me. I wanted to stop the horse and ask him what bothered him. I noticed Franchesca, who was still a black cat, walking alongside of Mage. She was staring at us and I believe she sensed what was wrong with Leo. Gordock then flew off my shoulder and began flying ahead of us. He flew over the trees, but stayed within range of my sight.

Before I knew it, we had arrived at a beach. Gordock flew around the water while I stopped Mage to jump off. It was beautiful here on the ocean, but just a bit cold. I saw a small shack that was hidden under some trees at the end of the beach, anchored beyond the dock was a large ship that stretched out into the ocean water. *A ship? I wonder if it belongs to someone here?* To the left of me was a carved wooden sign that said, *Hermit's Beach.* As we approached it, tall beyond muscular man came out. He was shirtless and wearing some type of cloth on his head. He had brown skin and dark eyes; his hair was long, coffee-colored, and hanging over his shoulders. He was wearing a pair of scarlet baggy pants tucked into black leather boots.

He looked about 30 and strikingly handsome. He had a sword attached to the large, gold belt around his waist. Around his neck was a thick, golden chain with a circular pendant attached to it. He walked up to us slowly and I noticed his hand moving over to his weapon. I expected him to react this way at first; I was dressed like a dark, evil sorcerer with a sword. Plus, Gordock flew back to my shoulder and did not help me look any kinder. In addition, Leo with his black leather and black hair made him seem just as evil as me. As for problem number four, well, the large black cat by our side was of no help to a friendly greeting. I then looked at everyone and began laughing out loud, which was very rude of me and I noticed Leo and Franchesca were staring at me as well.

"My prince, why are you laughing?" Leo asked, startled at my sudden outburst. I covered my mouth with my hand and continued to chuckle under my breath, "I am sorry, it's just… some jokes are just for me."

I stopped laughing after another entire minute. The man stood there in disbelief and thinking us as a bunch of fools, thanks to me. Even Mage looked like a dark and evil steed next to us, making me chortle as I passed him to approach the man. Bowing, I greeted him.

"Hello, dear friend. My name is Kain, I am the brother of Prince Abel," I announced. My hair was blowing around insanely from the ocean breeze and it was driving me mad. I pointed over to everyone watching us. "Those are my companions. The man on my horse, Mage, is my friend Leo. He is one of my brother's most powerful knights. The panther is named Franchesca and she will not hurt you." Gordock then made a noise with his beak and began flapping his wings. "Oh of course, how could I forget?" I began laughing, "This is also my trusted friend, Gordock." I smiled at the man who could only stare at such a strange looking group as us. His mouth was ajar and his hand began to move away from his sword.

"We are on a quest. We need to head southeast, which points us in the direction of the ocean. Do you know what could possibly be in that direction?" I added. He then took another look at all of us as we smiled at him. He shook his head.

"Southeast? Only the Forbidden Island is there. No sailor would ever head in that direction from this point; he would be mad! I mean, I am a brave sailor and have a fine ship, but no money in the world could make me sail there," He spoke. I grinned and pulled out a large pouch filled with gold coins. I handed it to him.

"Really?" I said to him with a hint of charm. The man looked at me confused and with a sparkle in his eye.

"Then call me crazy. Follow me!" he declared joyfully. He then began laughing and counting the gold coins. I looked over at everyone who was still watching and I nodded with a big grin. My teeth were showing perfectly as the man began walking back into his shack. He then noticed we did not follow him.

"What are you waiting for? Come in! Come in, please!" he shouted joyfully.

I ran up to Leo who still stared in a strange daze at me. I pulled him off Mage and told him to come in. "Let's go, handsome…he wants us to follow." I whispered. "He said he will take us! Stop staring, you look like a buffoon!" He continued to stare at me in a daze and I smiled at him. *What was wrong with him?*

"Leo, are you not feeling well? Did you not hear what I said?" I asked. He continued to stare and I tried to shake him out of his daze. He then looked downward. I grabbed his hand and pulled him over to the man's shack. We entered the beachside hut while Franchesca, Mage, and Gordock waited outside in the sand. The sun shined down on them, keeping them warm from the ocean breeze. The man's house was filled with fishing tools and stuffed fish that were mounted on the wall and tacked to wooden boards. He then turned to us and put the money away into a locked wooden cupboard.

"I hope you know we cannot leave today. It is very late and we must set forth tomorrow in the morning. There will be a storm tonight and that will make it difficult to sail." He was correct. After a long day's journeying, my companions and I had grown exhausted as well. I knew Leo was also hungry because I could hear his stomach growling. I saw him look down at it and I began to chuckle.

"I see my friends are hungry…I would not mind at all if we shared dinner, since you are staying the night as well," he said generously.

"Do you have a handkerchief or perhaps a ribbon that I can tie my hair back with? The loose strands are driving me mad," I admitted. I then smiled and looked down, thinking of how stupid I was to ask such a question. The man laughed, tilting his head back and such a deep laugh it was.

He took off the handkerchief that was on his head and said, "Here you go, my friend. You can keep it." The man smiled kindly and I beamed back at him.

"Thank you so much… are you sure you do not want it back? It is very pretty." I replied. He smiled at me.

"It's quite all right…I have many of them. Plus, you need something pretty for such lovely hair as yours," He said silkily. I bowed my head and found myself blushing like a fool. I then heard Leo walk out of the house and I quickly turned my back to the door.

"What's wrong with your friend?" The man said. I shook my head.

"I am sorry, I will be right back," I said to him while sprinting out the door. I saw that Franchesca was not on the sand anymore. I yelled for Leo, but I heard nothing. I could not see him anywhere.

"What is going on?" I whispered. I ran into the forest behind the house and there was a large rock in an opened area. On top of it was Franchesca, swinging her tail. Gordock flew over to my shoulder from his perch next to her. I walked quietly over to the stone and on the ground behind it was Leo. I looked at him with his knees drawn up to his chest like a small boy lost in his sadness. *What was wrong with him?* I walked around and sat next to him. Franchesca left us alone and I watched her walk away. I then turned my attention completely on Leo.

"Leo, my friend, what's wrong?" I inquired. He did not answer me at all and just turned his head away from me. *Why did he do this?* I took his hand and held it close to my chest. I wanted to take away whatever pain he felt.

"Do you miss someone? Perhaps my brother? Leo? Answer me… please?" I continued. He then turned his head to look directly at me. His eyes were filled with innocence and deep sadness. I felt his hand touch my cheek softly and I noticed a tear fall from his green eye.

"Leo…why do you cry?" I asked tenderly. It was killing me, how he was so silent. I wanted to see the old Leo. I felt myself begin to cry. Leo remained speechless, but rubbed his thumb up and down my cheek. *Did he think I could read his thoughts? Can my brother read people's thoughts?* I tried to dig into his mind, closing my eyes and concentrating on trying to pick up something, anything that may tell me what he was thinking or even feeling. I touched his cheek with my other hand, as he did with me. I felt him staring at me with those eyes while mine welled up with tears. I heard something from him. *Was it in his mind or did he say it?* I thought heard the word… *Love.*

"What?" I asked and I noticed he looked at me strangely. Did he say that? "Leo, did you just say something to me?"

"No," he said in a small whisper, his eyes looking confused.

I stared at him with the same confusion and thought I was losing my mind. *Why did I hear him say the word, "love?"* I looked down and gave up on trying to read into his thoughts. My hand slid slowly down from his face and to his chest. I leaned back on the rock, drawing my knees up the way he did. *Now who was the sad one?* Leo moved closer to me and I noticed he slid his arm around me. He held me and pulled me next to him.

"Kain? Why do you try to be so nice to me? You do not care about me, you just use me and I let you because I-" he stammered. My ears almost bled to what he just said and I turned to him, completely facing him.

"What?! What did you just say?!" I replied, outraged. He then felt my anger and backed slowly away from me. I continued, "You say I do not care about you and wish to only use you?! How dare you! What is drilling your head with such nonsense!?" I folded my arms and my eyebrows covered my eyes again.

"It's true, Kain… Everyone knows you are not allowed to love anyone," Leo sobbed. I sat there and almost in a way wanted to kill him for his insolence.

"What!? That is not true! It is a lie…a complete lie!" I screamed. I grabbed him and forcefully pushed him up against the rock.

"You see Kain, through the time I have known you, I have developed a…" he stopped for a minute and put his head down.

"You have developed a what!?" I yelled at him. He then looked back at me with the saddest eyes I have ever seen.

"I developed a- a love for you." He said, in almost a whisper. My anger faded away and my eyes softened, along with my face. I could not believe what he just said.

"What? You love me?" I said to him with a much softer voice, "But why? I mean..." I put my head down and let go of him from the wall.

"You see, Kain... this is why I am sad, because I know you will never love me in return. It is written in stone that you will never love anyone because you are the man who was chosen by Sceptor," He replied. I stared at him and then closed my eyes. That cannot be true because I have learned through my meeting with Abel that I can love. I discovered that love is greater than any other force in the world. I knew that there is nothing more important than being with the ones that love you.

Why does he say this? It cannot be true what he is saying, I passionately thought to myself. I opened my eyes and stared at him, and then, moving closer to him, I kissed his cheek. I moved my lips over to his ear and whispered softly to him, "I love you, Leo…"

I then moved back a bit so I could see his face. He was in shock, but I also noticed his eyes were closed. I then touched his cheek and said softly to him, "Leo, I can love, I can love anyone I wish. I have discovered the truth about life. Sceptor may have chosen me to be his dark puppet, but I will not allow him to control my strings. I control my own heart and what I know is that... I love you. You have only been kind to help me on my quest and such lovely company. Leo, I would give up my life for you. Please believe me when I say I love you," I declared.

I wanted to kiss him again as well as hold him tight. He lifted my hand and kissed it gently. I watched him with a smile on my face. I did love him and I could care less what anyone says. Oh, how I wanted him to hug me.

"Embrace me, Leo... please." *Did I say that out loud or was I just thinking that?* He must have heard it because I felt his arms come around me. I felt him pull me close and it felt soothing to be held by him. I did not want to let him go. I noticed Gordock must have flown away from my shoulder because he was no longer there. Leo and I must have held each other for the longest time because I saw the sun beginning to go down. I then heard the sailor calling our names with a torch in his hand. It was growing dark. Leo and I quickly let go of each other at the sound of his voice, and before I knew it, the man was standing right over us. I felt that my face was wet with tears, so I wiped them away forcefully.

"What are two doing out here?" the man said, laughing at the same time, "Come my friends, dinner is ready and I hope you like it." A cheerful smile spread across his face.

Leo and I both smiled at one another and we got up. I helped Leo stand to his feet, holding his arm. I did not let go of his arm as we walked over to the man's hut. Mage was still in the same spot I left him and Franchesca was now in the sand, resting at the spot where the man had a chair. He must have been out there speaking to her. I saw Gordock sitting on the back of the chair.

The beach was beautiful as the sun was setting. The sky was pink and the air was fresh. *Who would not want to live in such a beautiful place?* We walked into the house and sat down at the small table. There was a type of a fish on the table that looked extremely delicious along with loaves of fresh bread and wine. How kind it was for him to allow us to join him for such a meal. He had even made beds for us, which was also thoughtful of him. I noticed that Leo was watching me the entire time.

"So, what is your name? I asked the dark-skinned man. I forgot to tie back my hair, so I pulled out the handkerchief and then tied it back carefully.

"How rude of me! I never did introduce myself, did I? Well, my name is Tobit," he said as he smiled and continued eating his food. By now, my hair was neatly tied back. I felt far better and relaxed once my hair was off my shoulders. I stared, then looked at Leo and saw he was staring at me while he ate. *Why did he do that?* It did not matter to me, for he was adorable when he did.

"Tobit? Do you know what exactly is on this Forbidden Island?" I asked him politely. Everyone's heads rose up to look in Tobit's direction. A few strands of my bangs fell in front of my eyes as I waited for his response.

"Well, it is said to be guarded by a large red beast. It's known to be extremely powerful and destroys anything that comes near its treasure. It lives in a white cave at the top of the island's volcano. There also happens to be a religious cult that inhabits the land. No mortal man would wish to go there; I can only take you so far and wish you luck. Hell no am I taking you any further than that! I'll stay on the ship until you're done with your business there. If you don't return within two days, I'm heading out!" He explained. Leo dropped his fork, catching of all our attention.

"So, wait a minute, we are heading to an island that inhabits a crazy religious cult and a giant beast that lives in a volcano which could erupt at *any* minute?!

May I ask why we are doing this again?" Leo asked with a shaky voice.

"Oh Leo, you worry too much! We need to follow where the compass leads us. The island is our next destination. I am sure it isn't as bad as it is rumored to be. We'll get there and it should be smooth sailing. Trust me." I mentioned, playing with my food.

"Oh really? I am putting my trust in you Kain, I honestly hope you are correct. I don't want to die being eaten alive by some crazed giant beast or a cult of zealots! I love how you sit there and not fear the dangers of the world, but you had better be right!" He demanded, pointing his fork in my direction and waving it about like a mad man.

"Calm down, calm down." I laughed at him and then yawned. "You're working yourself up into a fit. No need to worry, let's get some rest and stop all this hogwash!"

"As crazy as I think you all are, we really should get some sleep before heading out on our dangerous journey," Tobit grumbled with a slight chuckle. He got up from his chair and walked over to his bed. "I made you all beds to sleep in. They are not fit for a prince, but they're the best I could do." He said as he burst into a jolly laughing fit.

"That is quite all right. As long as we have a roof over our head, I am sure things will be fine. Thank you for your trouble and wonderful help." I said to him.

"Goodnight, my friends. You're welcome, Kain." He replied kindly. I smiled and grabbed Leo's arm.

"Come to bed, Leo…" I whispered with a grin on my face. He smiled back and walked over with me to our beds. They were close together and on the floor. We had pillows, which were all I needed for a good night's rest. Leo got under the blanket that we both had to share. I lay down next to him under the blanket. It was comfortable… I was sleeping on my side, facing Leo. I then closed my eyes and at that moment, I felt an arm come around my waist under the blanket. I opened my eyes and saw Leo smiling with his eyes closed. I shook my head and beamed, closing my eyes.

Chapter Seven
Secrets of the Sea

When we had awoken in the morning, the sun shined through so harshly that I could see the pieces of dust that surrounded us. It was just chilly and Leo was still waking up when I looked at him. I noticed that Tobit was not there in his bed. In fact, he had already left the house. I got up and left Leo to wake up on his own. I walked out the door and I saw a large ship at the dock. There was an enormous white sail on it and it had a detailed design of a dragon head in the front of it. It was beautiful and I could not wait to begin our adventure. I stood at the doorway and I felt two arms come around me from behind. I turned and saw Leo was finally up from his restful sleep.

"Leo, what are you doing?" I said, laughing.

"Nothing, Kain…just greeting you a good morning," He said charmingly. Well, he sure did make it a good morning.

"Stop acting like a silly fool," I said, slapping his chest softly with my hand and laughing at the same time. "You can be so adorable when you want. Do you know that?" I continued, winking at him. He just stood there with a strange smile on his face. I saw him put his boots on and he looked at me one more time. He ran out the door to see the large ship and almost tripped on Franchesca. At least my Leo was back to his old self again. That made me happy to know he was content. I ran out after him and patted Franchesca on the head.

"My goodness, Franchesca, Leo almost stepped on you," I said, laughing charmingly. She licked my hand and I smiled down at her. I was looking for Gordock when I noticed that he was sitting on Mage's head. I laughed out loud because it looked foolish and cute. I then walked up to Tobit's ship as he spotted both Leo and I.

"Hey! Come on, you guys! The ship is almost ready. Come aboard and help me finish with the sails. The wind sure is kicking in beautifully today!" Tobit exclaimed with an upbeat tone of voice. I then wondered if I should bring Mage. I walked up to Leo and grabbed his shirt before he walked up on the ship.

"Leo, do you think I should bring Mage?" I asked. He then looked at me, smiling as usual. Why did he smile at me like that? I then felt him kiss my cheek. I just stared at him strangely and then smiled, bowing my head. Why did he do such things? "Leo, are you going to answer my question or just stand there staring at me all day?"

He then laughed softly to himself and said, "I am going to stand here all day staring at you. Do you have a problem with that?" I then looked at him almost in a daze.

"What..." I said to him, getting closer, "You better answer my question, smart one." I finished jokingly.

"And what if I don't, my prince?" He asked playfully. I stared at him and could not believe the game he was playing with me.

"What is it you are up to, Leo? Leo? Is there something spinning in that handsome brain of yours?" I said to him with a sly smile. He gazed at me with the same smile as if to mock me on purpose.

"You would not want to know what goes on in my brain, Kain." He said with a grin. My Gods, he did not know when to stop. He wanted to play this game with me all day. I moved his bangs away from his eyes and behind his ear.

"Leo, I do not know what I am going to do with you. I do not know who is crazier, you or the old woman in the forest?" I remarked and smiled at him, turning to face the ship. As I was about to climb aboard, I felt a large, strong hand grab my arm. Leo pulled me over to him and continued to stare at me. "Leo! Let me go!" I screeched, hitting his chest softly with my hand. He was grinning wider as I watched him. *Was he enjoying this*? "Leo we have to get going and-" I was interrupted by a kiss on my cheek, which was suspiciously close to my lips. I then pulled away from him slowly and hit his chest again, this time a bit harder. "What on Noven are you doing, Leo?" I said to him, whispering so Tobit did not hear us. He just looked down and tried to look innocent. "Do not even try to look innocent, Leo; it will not work this time! Now come on and stop fooling around!" I was deadly serious and he loved it. I could feel him grinning behind me as I took his hand, leading him up aboard the ship.

I decided then that I would tell Mage to stay in my brother's kingdom until I returned. I glided my way over toward my trusty steed, touched his cheek, and rubbed his nose gently. I focused thoughts of my brother's kingdom and telepathically told him to go there and wait for my return. Mage let out a neigh, kicked his hooves, and kneeled to me, bowing his head gracefully in respect for my command. Obeying it, he rode into the dark forest.

I made my way back upon the ship. Leo walked up to Tobit and helped him hold the rope as I stood there, watching them. *Like I was going to do that type of work*, I thought in a huff. *They have another thing coming if they think I am going to do labor like that*. I noticed something about Leo: he had been talking more. He usually was shy with me and other people. I heard him and Tobit laughing and talking together. Since last night, he had been more open and turning into a bit of a joker, not like I did not like that about him. At least I knew he had personality. I laughed softly to myself, folding my arms across my chest, watching them.

"Kain, why don't you come and help us?" Leo said with a huge grin on his face. I shook my head in defiance. The sun was bright and glaring in my eyes. My eyes were very sensitive, as well as my skin. I called for Franchesca to come aboard because we needed her with us. Her large paws climbed on deck and she walked up to me.

"You know, this is going to be fun, Franchesca. I cannot wait until we reach the island. I began wondering if Franchesca could talk. "Franchesca? Can you talk to us?" I asked while patting her. It did sound foolish, until I heard her voice.

"Of course I can." She said to me soothingly. My eyes widened.

"Well, why did you not talk to us before?" I inquired.

She looked up at me and spoke again, "What did I have to say? You never spoke to me until now. Plus, I did not want to interrupt your conversations with Leo." I had no idea she could talk and I began wondering if Leo knew she could.

"Does Leo know you can talk?" I inquired curiously.

"Yes he knows; I was talking to him yesterday evening on the rock," She said nonchalantly. She then looked over at Leo and whispered softly to me, "Leo has many feelings for you, Kain. He told me he cares about you and that he would give his life up for you. He said he had feelings for you like no other he has ever known, not even your brother." All I could do was stare at her and then at Leo.

"What kind of feelings? You mean…he loves me? Right?" I said with curiosity.

"Well, he did say he loves you-" she cut herself off; she was not telling me everything. "Well, maybe a bit more than that," she finished tactfully. I then stared at her directly.

"Please tell me what he said," I insisted, my heart beating faster and faster.

"He said he loves you like no one he had ever loved," she remarked. My face dropped and I almost felt myself faint... when oh yes, I did faint.

I was awakened by Leo tapping my face gently. I noticed I was not above deck, but down in the bunk. I stared at him, still trying to open my eyes. "Leo?" I whispered and I felt him kiss my cheek.

"Yes, my prince... do not worry... I am here, I am here." He said softly against my cheek. I wrapped my arms around his waist and held him close to me. I just laid there embracing him. I did not want to let him go. I then moved so I could look at him with a smile. He beamed back at me. "Are you all right, Kain?" He said with the kindest, softest voice.

"Yes, I am, Leo," I replied. I kissed his cheek. "It must have been the sun. I am very fragile beneath it..."

"We have already set sail, my prince. Tobit is controlling the ship above deck. He said that tonight, there is going to be a storm, so he has to stay up late and navigate," He said. I then nodded at him and smiled.

"Well, I hope everything works well tonight. I cannot wait until we get to the island," I remarked. Leo looked charmingly handsome. I could not dare look at him anymore or else I would faint again. *What is it I feel for him?* I mused. *Why do I continue to stare at him and love him for his kindness? This is a me I never thought I was. I used to hate and hurt, but now I love and give. The power of the Dark God must be breaking loose from me. I shall have no one rule me, no matter who they are or what they do. I was born with royal blood and therefore I could care less about any pathetic God. I shall rescue my brother from my master Ariaus, find the Sword Nebula and destroy whatever evil dares to stop me!* I got up from where I was laying and touched Leo's cheek. I walked up the stairs to the top part of the ship. I then saw Franchesca and Gordock next to Tobit. I walked over to Tobit and touched his shoulder.

"How is the ship doing, my friend?" I inquired.

"We're faring well so far, though who knows out in an ocean like this what will happen," Tobit exclaimed with a grin. I nodded what he said and then looked up and saw the stars and how beautiful they looked. I slid my hand off Tobit's shoulder, but as I did, I heard a large bang.

"What the hell was that!?" I shouted to Tobit.

Tobit then yelled out, "I don't know what that was! Go down below, Prince Kain! Now!"

I then bellowed back to him, "No, Tobit! Are you mad? I will not leave you up here alone!" I felt the ship shake again and I noticed Tobit was struggling to control it.

"Kain! You better do as I say!" He insisted. I then saw Leo run up the stairs and Franchesca ran up to him.

"Are you alright, Leo?" Franchesca asked, frightened. Leo nodded and ran up to me.

"My Prince! Are you alright?" Leo asked. He then hugged me and touched my shoulders.

"Yes, I am fine. Thank you for asking. Leo, I want you to get down below, for me and Tobit will stay above and see what happened," I explained. Leo then withdrew his sword.

"No Kain, I will not leave you!" He exclaimed.

"Leo, you will do as I command! Now go!" I demanded. Tobit turned his head with his hands still gripped tightly upon the wheel.

"How about both of you go down below and let me handle this!" He shouted. Leo and I both looked at Tobit then looked at each other. I nodded at Leo and took his arm. Franchesca was behind us and Gordock landed clumsily upon my shoulder. I led Leo and Franchesca to the lower level. When we reached the bottom, I felt the ship shake from something enormous slamming against it.

"My Prince, what is that?" Leo asked in fright. I then looked over at him; he was holding onto the wall of the ship.

"I don't know, Leo... If I did, I would tell you," I said. He then held onto my arm.

"Maybe it's a monster or another ship trying to hit us," he suggested shakily. I then looked at him.

"There is no monster that dares to tangle with me. I will not let anything hurt you or anyone," I said to Leo in a soft voice. I then felt the ship tilt all the way to the right. All of us fell over and slid up against the wall. "That's it! I am going to see what this is all about!" I shouted. I felt Leo grab my arm again.

"Kain, please do not go up there!" He pleaded. I looked at him with my eyebrows together covering my eyes with a shadow.

"Let... me... go! You cannot stop me!" I then pushed him, but with shocking strength, he flew farther than I thought. Franchesca stared at me, then at Leo. I felt the ship rock again and ran up above. I saw that Tobit had his sword in his hand and was trying to control the ship at the same time. I ran up next to him with my hair falling apart and blowing in the wind. I put my hands up on his shoulders. "What is going on!?"

I yelled. The winds were strong and pushing the ship from side to side.

"There is something large trying to attack our ship!" Tobit shouted back. I looked at him, then the water. The waves were crashing over on us, soaking the deck. I could not believe we were in the heart of a storm along with an unknown force trying to attack us.

"What could it be!?" I screamed again.

"I believe it could be a whale!" Tobit bellowed. I grabbed on to the side of the ship and peered into the water. I then noticed a massive shadow coming to the surface. It did not look like any whale to me. Two horns poked out, then an enormous, dark blue, monstrous head with fangs the size of a man's leg. This creature was colossal, snakelike, and the neck began to rise along with two hands.

"My Gods! It's a dragon!" I cried in disbelief.

Staring at the thing in shock, I heard Tobit yell out, "In the name of Vertigo! That is a Water Dragon! We will never get out of this alive!" I then shook my head and saw the dragon come closer, exhaling its hot breath on me. My hair was blowing and my mouth was closed tight, along with my eyes. When I opened them, I saw the dragon had exposed its mouth. I could smell the ocean from his breath, a more powerful stench than the sea itself. I thought for sure I was going to die. I looked down and closed my eyes. What was I doing? I had the power of a God and here I feared a dragon?

I then opened my eyes devilishly and grinned. I raised my arms in the air and yelled out cabalistic words, "Kia bla du shantoo... de bunda ka bele!" To my amazement, the water rose around us in a circle. The purple stone upon my chest began to glow and the dragon's eyes turned purple as well. I continued to grin and watched the dragon roar and shake his head. His large clawed hands scratched its nose. The dragon then lit up in purple. The lavender light glowed around him and also from within him. The dragon was confused as I began controlling his mind. "Go back and leave us Dragon, for my power is too great for you! I shall take your soul if you dare come near this ship! Be gone and leave us!" I commanded. The dragon then slid back below the ocean. I turned my head and realized that Tobit was watching me the entire time. He could not believe his eyes. I then turned slowly around and stared at my friend and walked over to him. I felt incredibly powerful and also quite... evil. It must have been the ability within me that made me feel that way, so very devilish and drowning in my own power.

I touched Tobit's shoulder again and asked him quietly in his ear, "Are you all right, my friend?" He just stared at me, then took my hand and kissed it. I watched him do this and could not understand why.

"You are a God, I shall do anything you wish, Prince Kain. One who can frighten away a dragon has the power of a deity," Tobit remarked with wonder. I shot him a grin. *A power of a God indeed, but what does he know of my power? If he were to know I was given the abilities of the dark God Sceptor, then would he do whatever I wished? I think not!* I continued to smile at him and noticed to the left of me, Leo and Franchesca were also watching. I smiled at them and looked over at Tobit.

"My friend, I do believe you have a ship to steer. Even though the dragon is gone, we still have a storm to get through," I said with a chuckle. Hours passed before the storm finally gave in and the night sky had returned along with the stars. Tobit navigated us through excellently with his skill of controlling the ship. I was exhausted and wished to get some sleep. Leo was shocked from what happened. I walked over to him and smiled.

"You okay, Leo?" I asked with concern. He stared at me with his bright green eyes. I took his arm and led him down to the bunk. There was a bed down there and I sat him down on it. I settled down next to him. *Why did he silently stare at me?* I then felt his hand brush a strand of my long wavy hair away from my eyes. He was gentle and his skin was warm. I then looked down and took his hand. "Leo, why do you treat me this way? Why is it you stare at me?" I asked. He sat there silently and blinked.

"Oh…I am sorry if I stare at you, Kain; I daydream at times," He said softly. I looked at him, and then turned my head down.

"It seems you always daydream when you stare at me. That does not explain why you treat me this way," I said to him, licking the top part of my teeth. I was still holding his hand, awaiting his response.

"Kain, I just wish to serve you as my prince. I-" He stammered. I then stopped him by putting my finger on his lips.

"Shh... no more... you treat me like no man has ever treated me. Not even a woman has treated me so well. I have never been treated so kindly other than by my own brother." I admitted, lowering my head. "Franchesca told me something. She said that you love me more than anyone you have ever loved. How is this possible?" I asked him, looking back into his eyes. I saw his gaze move around the room as if he was too ashamed to look straight at me. I then moved my hand over to his face and rubbed his cheek with my thumb. "Look at me, Leo," I instructed smoothly, "Look at me... I want you to answer me, even if this will take all night. You will answer me..." I whispered. He then looked at me and continued to stare with that usual look upon his face.

"It is true, my prince..." he replied at last. My eyes were shaded in darkness, making me look quite devilish.

"Leo, how is this possible? You mean to tell me that you love me more than anyone you have ever loved? More than even a woman you have perhaps fallen in love with before? More than my brother?" I asked him, bewildered. He peered into my eyes silently, but I wanted answers. "Leo! Answer me now!" I demanded. I was losing my patience with him.

"Yes," he said so softly to me.

"Yes what!? What does this *yes* mean?" I snapped, becoming more frustrated.

"Yes, that I love you more than anyone. I do not know why... I just do. Please, my prince, I am tired. I wish to sleep. Perhaps we will speak of this some other time. Forgive me." He said, taking my hand and kissing it. He then started to open his black leather coat. I folded my arms, staring at him with my eyes wide open, my bottom lip just a bit lowered to show my teeth. I was shocked at how he can end a conversation so quickly about such a subject. I wanted to grab him, shake him, and slap him about, but I could not find the evil in me to do it. *What could I do now*?

"So that's all? That's all you have to say?" I asked with frustration. He turned to face me and nodded. I looked to my side and had an idea. I moved closer to him and helped him untie his black shirt. He then looked up at me and watched me.

"Kain... what are you doing? I can handle this. Now, you go off to sleep because I know you are..." He said to me so very softly. I then shushed him with my finger on his lips again.

"No more... I am sorry." I moved my lips up to his, letting my upper and bottom lip barely touch his, feeling his hot breath glide into my mouth. "Leo..." I whispered to him, pressing my body closer to his, kissing his masculine lips. I gazed sweetly into his eyes right before I kissed him. He sat there, watching me with his eyes half closed. I kissed his lips softly and slid my hand over to his cheek. I felt him begin to kiss me back. I was melting; if only this could have lasted forever. I felt him take my hand away from his face. He slid his fingers through mine and kissed me passionately. My heart was racing wildly. *Why was I loving this from him? I loved him and I never wanted to stop loving him. Why was it I fancied men in such a way?* My eyes were closed and I felt his arm slide behind my back, pushing me closer to him. *Oh Gods, please don't stop*. Did I say that out loud or was I just thinking that?

While I was lost in the moment, the door suddenly opened and Tobit walked in the room. Leo quickly let go of me and I almost fell to the floor. I was breathing heavy and my mind was still muddled. Leo looked away to the small round window.

"Wha?! I don't know what I just walked into, but I sure am sorry, whatever it was I walked into." Tobit exclaimed, and then walked back up the stairs, shutting the door behind him. I looked at Leo and noticed he was already looking at me.

"By the Gods! What do you think Tobit is thinking right now?" I blurted nervously, biting my nails. He sat there and folded his arms. I then thought I saw him chuckle under his breath.

I looked at him closer and said, "Leo, are you laughing?" I held back a chuckle myself.

"Yes..." He replied, now laughing even louder. I stared at him and held my stomach, giving into the humor. Leo laid down on the bed and was snickering so loudly that he had put the pillow over his face. I laughed uncontrollably, which made me tumble off the bed and land straight down on the floor. I cackled even harder, thinking of what I just did and how stupid I looked.

"Can... can... you imagine... just... what he is thinking?! My Gods... did you see his face?!" I managed to say while rolling around on the floor. I saw Leo almost fall off the bed with me, his face turning completely red. I then climbed back up on the bed and Leo was now trying hard to stop laughing, as well as I. I climbed up next to him, at last more relaxed at the thought and laid there on my back. Leo was calmer as well, lying in the same position next to me. It was comfortable, laying there, even though the bed was small but somehow it was a wonderful feeling to be squished next to him. Leo was now completely calm and spooned up against me, holding me from behind.

He began telling me that he will never leave my side and this was the most exciting adventure he had ever been on. I had my eyes closed with a smile on my face. I loved listening to him. I felt him cover me because I believe he knew I was falling asleep. He laid there on his side, leaning on his elbow. I felt him touch my hair; he was sliding his fingers through it. It relaxed me. I was falling asleep to his soft words and tender touch. *Oh Leo, don't ever leave me...*

Chapter Eight
The Forbidden Island

When we had awakened, it was nearly midday. The air was cold down in the bunk and I had slept peacefully. Leo was right next to me with his long, black bangs covering the side of my cheek. He had his arm wrapped around me. He rustled and made a soft noise. How adorable. I smiled down at him and watched him while he slept. I was almost on top of him, brushing his bangs away from his face. I moved down to kiss his forehead. I then got up off the bed and put my belt back on along with my sword. I was ready to battle on any creature or monster that dared come near me. I then began thinking of my master again. *Just where was he and what was his plan*? I wondered to myself. I looked back at Leo and smiled, then ran up the stairs to the deck of the ship. Tobit was at the wheel and Franchesca was next to him. I then looked down, trying not to laugh, but was embarrassed as well. I did not know what he was going to say and I am sure Tobit was at a loss for words. I walked over to him and put my arms behind my back. I bowed down to pat Franchesca on the head.

"How was your sleep, my dear?" I asked. She purred and licked my hand.

"I slept peacefully knowing we have such a powerful man aboard with us," She said, winking at me with her large cat eye. I smiled down at her charmingly and then looked over at Tobit for a minute. Tobit stared straight ahead; he looked like he was trying to ignore me.

"I would like to apologize what happened last night, Kain. You see, I had no idea you and Leo... were... well, you know." He remarked, barely concealing the blush that crept upon his face. I then began to laugh rather rudely.

"My friend, it is quite all right, I assure you, I did not know myself until that very moment," I said to him quite charmingly.

"I have known men like you and your friend Leo. They are very nice, perhaps some of the kindest I have ever met," he replied with a sheepish grin. I then laughed softly to myself.

"Then you do not know me very well, my friend," I whispered into his ear slyly. I then grinned at him and laughed out loud, walking over to the end of the ship. Franchesca followed and stood next to me. I was looking over at the ocean thinking of Ariaus and the sword. "What would Ariaus do to my brother? If only I could stop everything right now and take him with me. I hope he is all right and not hurt," I said softly to Franchesca.

"Not to change the subject Prince Kain, but what exactly is it Tobit was sorry for?" She asked curiously. I then looked away for a moment.

"My dear, nothing important... really," I whispered. I then bit my lip and continued to look out at the ocean.

"Tobit said to me that you and Leo are secret lovers. Is this true? Do you only enjoy the company of men?" She inquired innocently, but also sadly.

"My Gods, slow down my dear. Who said I did not fancy women? And just what makes Tobit think Leo and I are lovers?" I said with my icy, blue eyes gazing fiercely at her. My wavy hair hung loosely over my shoulders and my bangs were in front of my eyes. I looked like an evil, terrifying pirate in this moment with the severe expression on my face, my black leather pants and boots, black leather vest and puffy cotton shirt. My hair was very long, longer than most women, yet with my sharp features, my locks managed to look rugged as well as beautiful. I noticed Franchesca stared at me in a strange, yet gentle way. I had a feeling she had fallen in love with me. I folded my arms and heard her speak.

"Well, I thought that since Tobit caught you and Leo kissing each other passionately that perhaps you two were secret lovers. The way Leo looks at you... it's just... well...you stare at him at times as well. And the way Leo spoke of love for you, it just seemed to-" She stuttered.

"I know. I can understand how you two can both think such things and yes, perhaps it is obvious. It does not mean I do not fancy women. I adore women and would oftentimes have wished to be with one. Trust me on that, but Leo and I had no idea about ourselves loving each other in such a way until now. I mean, we just met." I said to her softly.

"I see. My prince, please do not feel that it bothers me that you two love each other. I am happy for you both and I am grateful you both are taking me with you on this wonderful journey. It is very kind of you to help me gain my human self again. I hope the sword has the power to change me back," She said, lowering her head. Her words were sincere, yet I knew it hurt her to speak them.

"Of course it will! I will make sure of it. As long as we get there before my master does and gain the sword's power. This will be a challenge, for he is incredibly powerful. I do believe he has a gift from the dark God Sceptor as well as I do. He must have been given this gift to make sure that I fulfill my destiny. Though my fate is to collect the sword, who said I was going to use it for evil?" I said, grinning down at her. "I am not who I used to be. I was once a cruel and greedy man. I hope that never happens to me again. I am afraid that Sceptor has the ability to control me at any time he wishes. If that ever happens, you would have to destroy me. Can you promise me this?"

"Promise you this? How can I destroy you? I do not believe I could ever hurt you, prince Kain..." she said, the shadow of sadness in her eyes.

"When you see my evil side, you will wish me dead. Trust me, my beautiful one, you will," I said gravely. I then heard a loud voice yell from behind me.

"Land! I see The Forbidden Island! We're here! Get the anchor ready, we will be there soon!" Tobit yelled out with mirth in his voice. The poor guy had not slept a wink. I then saw Leo help him drop the sails and prepare the anchor. I then laughed to myself.

"Notice I always let Leo do all the hard work. I have not lifted a finger to help since we got on this ship. Am I lazy or just afraid of ruining my beautiful hands?" I wondered aloud. I snickered, noticing how feminine I sounded. I also noticed I was the only one laughing. "Oh, well, I thought it was funny." I said charmingly, staring at Franchesca with a grin. I patted her head and walked over to the front of the ship where I could see the island. My Gods, I was so excited and yet I knew I fibbed to Leo when telling him to trust me that the island wasn't dangerous, yet I couldn't help myself. My thirst for danger excited me! The wind blew in my face and I held my hands upon the edge of the ship. Franchesca stared at me strangely as she took notice of the large frightening grin upon my face. She knew then that it would be no smooth ride from here on out. She sensed the danger that lay ahead just as much as I did and I LOVED IT!

I was amazed that I had gotten this far and soon, the map would be mine! I pulled out the key that would open the chest ahead, the beautiful key with the compass head. As the boat neared land, I began to feel dizzy. *I will kiss whatever ground it is that the chest is placed on as soon as we dock. Once I get this map, I will have complete control on where this sword is. Then all that is left is getting through whatever lies ahead.* I thought of all this, staring at the island. After shaking my head to regain my senses, I ran up to Tobit and hugged him.

"Thank you, my strong friend! You have my gratitude for taking us here!" I exclaimed. He smiled a bit. I had forgotten of what he thought about me and began to laugh. Tobit smiled and I could see how weak he was from lack of sleep. I walked past Leo who hoisted the anchor on deck and readied it for landing. Brushing my long black hair off my shoulders, I felt exhausted, so I yawned near poor Tobit as Franchesca watched me and shook her head.

"I am bloody starving and *sooo* exhausted," I yawned and stretched again as I noticed my entire crew staring at me with frustration upon their faces. "What?" I said to them as Leo dropped anchor, annoyed. One by one, we all loaded onto the tiny rowboat the ship had tied in tow. My heart was beating with the rhythm of the oars that Tobit and Leo were rowing. My eyes were scanning the entire part of the island. Gordock had been sitting now on my shoulder and I felt the heat of the sun hit me like a flaming arrow. When we had finally arrived at the shore, I could not wait to make a fire and eat something.

It had to be nearly evening when we had made camp. Tobit caught us some fish and Leo was in charge of making the shelter. As for me, it only took a second to make the fire. I rubbed my palms together, mumbled cabalistic words of power, and watched as the flames sprouted on the kindling that Leo and Tobit had collected. I stood there laughing to myself and I felt Franchesca lay down next to my leg.

"You are a lazy bastard, Kain," she said, laughing to herself.

"Of course I am. I have royal blood in me, my dear. I do not slave for others, others slave for me," I declared. She shook her head in disbelief. I began laughing and she laughed along with me. I sat down next to her on the hot, white sand and the fire felt quite warm to be next to. Franchesca was also quite warm and her purring relaxed me. I laid my head on her back and I felt her tail stroke my face.

"You are quite handsome, my prince…do you realize this?" Franchesca pointed out. I then laughed softly.

"My dear, of course I notice. Oh, how you make me laugh." I said charmingly to her, resting my eyes.

"I am serious, prince... you are," she replied earnestly. I leaned into her ear to speak.

"You should talk, my lady... your beauty is devilishly striking. Even as a large, raven colored cat," I grinned as I spoke and I heard rich laughter from her. I believe I fell asleep for a bit, for I was awakened by Tobit roasting fish over the fire, who, mind you, hadn't slept in over 24 hours. I could have imagined his exhaustion, but I was busy sleeping. Leo was sitting next to me along with Franchesca, who was still stroking my face with her tail.

"Tobit my friend, you should sleep and get rest. You have not slept in two days," I remarked. Leo had already eaten some of the fish. I watched him and smiled. I was given some fish by Tobit. Leo ate like a barbarian while I ate like a pigeon.

"I had such a lovely nap! I dreamed of crystal unicorns and friendly dragons! It was quite lovely. Tobit, thank you for this meal, it is delicious! You are an amazing cook," I said to him as I nibbled on the fish.

"Kain, you are something else! I'm gonna start charging you by the hour!" He replied, chuckling to himself as he stoked the fire with more wood.

"You should really eat some more of this fish, Kain; it's quite delicious," Leo mumbled with his mouth full and holding a piece of it up to my face. I continued to look at him a little disgusted then smiled for it was quite cute.

"Leo I am fine with this fish, thank you," I insisted with a grin. I then ate a small piece of my fish and watched everyone else devour their food. While I sat, I thought I had heard a noise off in the distance of the island. I looked past the trees and flowers. What could that have been?

"Did anyone of you hear that?" I asked everyone. Leo shook his head as well as Tobit. I then thought perhaps I was just acting paranoid when I heard it again! This time, it was louder than before. I noticed Gordock was flying around in circles above us. I quickly turned around, looking for the creature that made such noises. "Now tell me if you didn't hear that?!" I said. I stood up and withdrew my sword. I noticed everyone else was quiet and waiting for something to happen. Leo had his hand on his sword and Tobit did the same. I scanned out as far as possible when I then saw a man dodge out from the trees. He carried a sword and began swinging it at me. I dodged from him and feeling the sword hit mine, we fought. He was a novice swordsman, but I was a master. Leo then charged after the man and frightened him. While Leo ran toward the man, I quickly stabbed him through the heart. As he fell to the ground, I heard three more men charge out from the dark bushes. Leo and I both turned to fight and I saw Franchesca run after one of the attackers. She pinned him down, tearing out his throat. Tobit then charged out after the man that was fighting

Leo and both of them fought together. More men began to charge out from the line of trees beyond the rocky beach.

"What the hell is going on!?" I yelled out, fighting a man clothed in a monk's attire. The men wore strange jewelry and dark robes.

"I have no idea, Kain!" Leo shouted back. I then ducked while the man swung his broadsword at me. He overreached and I stuck my sword in his gut, tearing open his flesh and watching the blood pour out onto the ground. My teeth were bared and my hair was making me look like a wild man. I watched another attacker come at me and I moved to the right as he tried to swing at me with his staff. I then darted to the left, but the movement was too slow and I felt a painful strike on my shoulder. I then looked up at him and ran after the man, grabbing him by his neck and pinning him against a tree. I was so lost in my anger that I actually had the amazing strength to throw this man across the sand. I was going mad and wanted to crush these fools into the ground.

More came and were attacking me from every corner. I grinned with a devilish look and began grabbing the men and cracking their spines over my knee. What was I doing? I was unstoppable with this power and it only grew stronger. My purple stone was glowing and the darkened sky now grew even darker. I was too fast for them, slicing my sword through them and ripping their hearts out with the palm of my hand. *What kind of a monster am I, to do such things to people?*

I saw that Leo and Tobit were still fighting and I walked up to the men that dared to come near them. I then pulled out a small knife I had in my boot and flung it at one of the men. It sliced straight through his neck and I smiled, watching him fall to the ground. Leo stared at me as I continued my work with the man that fought Tobit. From behind, I grabbed him by the back of his neck and wrapped my arm around his head, cracking his bones. The man fell before my feet and I just stood there grinning, still with the power flowing through my blood. I was lost in this power, turning to see if Franchesca was all right. I saw she was feasting on the man she had torn apart. Gordock then landed on my shoulder out of nowhere and began making strange noises. I then licked the blood from my sword and placed it back in its case. I pulled off a small ribbon from one of the dead men on the ground and I tied back my hair with it. My bangs were still in front of my eyes as I walked over to Leo.

"Are you all right, my sweet one?" I inquired with a grin. I then turned to Franchesca and Tobit as well. "Is everyone all right?" I asked.

"Yes, my prince." Leo said, kissing my hand.

"Yes," Franchesca and Tobit spoke at the same time. I walked over to Tobit and touched his shoulder.

"You are a great fighter, my friend." I said to him charmingly.

"I am?! You are unstoppable with that strength and speed of yours!" Tobit remarked with an expression of shock in his face.

"You are just as powerful as your brother, Kain," Leo said, putting his sword away.

"No! My brother is much more powerful than me. It is written in stone... he has the gift from Vertigo, the God of light. As for me, I have the gift from Sceptor, the dark God," I said, looking down and folding my arms. I could feel everyone staring at me and they knew who I was talking about.

"Your brother was given power by the God of light? And you were give power by the God of darkness? How is this possible? Are you working for

Sceptor and using us to help you gain true power, perhaps to destroy us all?! And this just seems to be all a trick to make me believe otherwise! I thought I sensed evil when I first saw you and your friends walk on my golden sand! I am leaving you all! To think that I helped the God of darkness!" He shouted angrily. He stormed over to the small rowboat, but right before he climbed in it, I grabbed him by his shoulder. "Let me go, you Warlock! Demon! Whatever you are!" Tobit commanded with fear in his eyes.

"Please silence yourself, Tobit. I wish not to harm you and I do not work for Sceptor. I may have been chosen by him to have this power, but it does not mean I will work for him! Please settle down, my friend. I do not wish harm on anyone, but those who are working for Sceptor. Leo! Help me explain this to him." I said, still holding his shoulder.

"It is true, Tobit, I work for his brother as a trusted knight. He wishes no harm and loves his brother very much. You must believe him," Leo said with a soft tone of voice. "Please believe me. I may look quite devilish at times, but I really am not like that," I added. He just stood there looking back and forth at Leo and me.

"Alright! I guess I can believe you. May the Gods help me for believing you, but I will go with my heart," Tobit concluded, walking back over to the small fire. I smiled at Leo for backing me up. Franchesca watched the entire scene, somewhere off in a darkened shadow.

"All right, now that we got that all taken care of, let's check one of the bodies of the men and see just whcrc thcy camc from and just what thcy want from us." I declared, walking over to one of the dead, darkly robed men. I knelt down to check under the robe of one of the men. I found a necklace with a strange pendant on it. When I looked closer, there was a symbol of a red dragon. What did this mean? I then checked the arm of the man and saw the same marking tattooed onto it. I then checked the other men and they all wore the same symbol. Leo walked over to me and he stared at the man by my feet.

"I know of who these men are and what purpose they serve. They are the Monks of The Red Dragon. They are the protectors of a red dragon that holds a special golden chest. My prince, I believe this dragon protects the map," Leo explained. I gawked at him. How does he just know these things all of a sudden?

"And you heard of this where?" I asked him, folding my arms.

"The elders spoke of it. They spoke of you and your brother, of the prophecies that are supposed to happen and how the planets are to form a pattern in the sky. This is all talk from the astrologers and the alchemist. The elders hold the secrets to what is going to happen. They say they were given a gift by Vertigo to know the future. If only I listened to them more; I never believed in their stories until I met you. They also told me when the prophecies will begin taking place, but I no longer remember the day and time. Whatever they said, I am sure this prophecy will happen soon," He responded, lowering his head.

"It's okay Leo, but the information that you have given me so far is plentiful," I said, smiling at him. I wanted to kiss him, but everyone was watching us. I walked over to the fireplace and pulled out my sword. I sat down and began sharpening it slowly.

"I will get this map and fight anything I must that dares to stand in my way," I proclaimed with a grin on my face.

"This map… what exactly does it do? Why do you need it, if you don't mind me asking?" Tobit asked curiously.

"Well, it's a bit of a long story, but for now, I will give you the short version." I mentioned as we all explained to Tobit the reason for obtaining the map, the sword, and how my master will use it for evil if he found it first.

"So this is why you all are so eager to go through this madness? Hm," He crossed his arms over his chest and held his chin as if in deep thought, then looked up at me. "Interesting. So it's your master who's evil and I'm supposed to trust that you are the good guys."

"YES!" We all responded at the same time.

"Alright, alright, I believe you, so let's get this thing and get the hell out of here!" He replied, waving his hands up in the air in defense. Everyone had walked over to me and sat down around the fire. Leo had withdrawn his sword and also began sharpening it. His face was smooth and handsome; I noticed myself staring at him. Franchesca was watching us both and noticed far before I did that I was staring at Leo.

"Leo?" I asked him. Tobit was watching us as well.

"Yes," Leo replied.

"Will my brother ever love me the way he used to?" I asked him kindly. Leo then looked up at me and saw my eyes. He saw that my eyes were glassy and gazed at me sadly. "He had thrown me out of his castle and told me I was not his brother anymore," I finished, looking down.

"I am sure he did not mean it, my prince. Abel is nothing like that and I am sure he still loves you. Give him time Kain, and he will understand. I am sure he has already made his decision and knows that you love him. When we find the sword, we will fix everything. He will understand." Leo said kindly to me, rubbing my back with his hand. I then put my sword down and leaned on his shoulder. I was comfortable and tired. I wanted to stay there with him all night.

He held me and brushed my hair away from my eyes. I could feel Franchesca and Tobit's gaze upon us, but I could care less and I knew it was more important to find out where these monks lived. It was not safe to sleep here. I then looked at Leo and kissed his cheek. Smiling at him, I got up from the sand, placing my sword away and turning toward Tobit.

"My friend, I believe you should sleep on your ship while Leo, Franchesca, and I find out where these monks live. Then, we can know how to get to the dragon," I said to him, smiling.

"Why would you want to go there? They will capture you and sacrifice you to the creature or maybe even kill you! Are you crazy, and all for a map?" Tobit snapped, folding his arms. I then began to laugh.

"Well my friend, if they try to sacrifice us to the dragon, we can then kill the dragon and find the chest. Plus, maybe the monks just might help us if we are polite enough." I said, laughing. "I am in the mood for danger and I will make sure nothing harms any one of you." I said, still laughing to myself and taking Leo's arm.

"You are crazy! How do you know that the dragon will not kill you!? How do you know you're gonna make it out of this!?" Tobit shouted.

"Shh... quiet, my friend. To answer your question, how will we ever know until we find out? We have no other choice. Now, go get some rest... please." I instructed. "If we do not return in three days, then leave this island."

"Leave you here? What if you're still alive in three days?" Tobit inquired.

"Just do as I say, please Tobit," I demanded, pulling Leo's arm harder, leading him to the tall trees.

"Alright, alright, calm your princely head. You have my word. May the Gods be with you," he said, dragging his small boat along the sands and into the sea.

I nodded and yelled back, "As well with you!" I let go of Leo's arm and walked in front of us. Gordock was already ahead and Franchesca stalked along in the back. Leo was chopping some of the large bushes as we walked on an overgrown pathway. Leo was frightened and I could sense it, but I could not wait to see the monks' hideout. I then could hear men talking in the distance, but saw nobody.

"Can you hear that, Leo?" I asked him. Leo just shook his head. "Can you hear those men talking, Franchesca?" I asked her.

"I thought I heard something, but I was not sure. You must have some powerful ears my prince, if you can hear things louder than I can, even in my panther form," She replied.

It must be this power I had within me, to see and hear better than I could ever before. *How amazing this is to have such a power. At this point, it is dark and I can still see without a torch or some type of light. This power in me must be getting stronger by the day. The Gods only know how far away those men are*, I thought. We continued our way through until I saw torches.

"Stop," I said quietly, "I see torches ahead. That must be were their temple is." I spied their grand structure. It was rectangular at the bottom level, above which rose into the sky in a pyramidal shape. Each of the gigantic stone bricks from which the building was constructed was painted in a deep red-orange hue. It was lit on all sides with tall torches and the entrance was guarded by twin dragon sculptures, their mouths carved open and spewing out stone flames. I then moved closer to the small lights that circled this large building. Staying hidden behind the bushes with Leo, Franchesca growled behind me.

I noticed a long line of the monks walking out of the temple. They stood in a line with their heads bowed. Each one held a torch and a sword. There were two monks that began playing deep-sounding drums. At the entrance, another robed man had appeared, but he was not like the others; he was not wearing a hood. This man wore a mask and his robe was blood red. It seemed this man wore a wig as well, for the hair was curled out impossibly high into the air. *He must be the leader,* I thought. The color of his hairpiece was also blood red and the mask was shaped like a dragon's head. This had to be the beginning of a strange cultist ritual.

"You must search out and find these mortals who dare disturb the dragon and steal the map from its holy place! Now go! Find them and return them to me!" He commanded.

"*Well*, so much for asking them to help us, *Kain*! Now they want us dead!" whispered Leo as he looked at me with frustration.

I wanted to laugh, but I would have made too much noise. Holding back my laughter, avoiding to make too much noise, I had hoped for the monks to search out into the forest, and then gestured for Leo and Franchesca to follow me. I ran up to the temple and hid up against the wall in a shadow. Leo was next to me and Franchesca was low to the ground, ready to pounce. I was now looking through one of the large dragon statues that guarded the stairs and saw the master turn, walking back inside. I then came up with a wonderful idea. We needed robes to sneak in and find out where the dragon was, so I ran back over to the bushes and hid behind them. Leo and Franchesca followed silently behind me.

"I have a plan, my friends, we will go back to the beach and take the robes of the men that we killed. We must move quickly before they find them there," I explained.

When we reached the beach, not a living soul was present. Even Tobit's ship was a safe distance away and hidden by the night sky. Sensing it was safe, I grabbed one of the bodies and pulled off his robe while Leo did the same. After hiding the corpses in the brush by the forest, I looked at Franchesca and formulated a plan for her.

"Franchesca, you will hide in the bushes next to the temple, while Leo and I go in and find out where the dragon is located. Do you understand?" I asked her kindly.

"Yes, my prince. I understand." She said, nodding. I was now hidden in the robe, as well as Leo.

"You look dashing in that robe, Leo," I said to him, grinning and turning my back on him. I then looked back and saw Leo shake his head. I laughed softly to myself, noticing that Franchesca was also shaking her head. Walking back into the woods with Leo and Franchesca behind me, I felt a chill growing in the air. We finally reached the temple after a silent walk through the woods. We ran quickly to the wall and ducked down behind the statue again.

"Okay Franchesca, you stay here in this shadow and watch what happens until we come out," I whispered to her. I then saw a few robed men walk up to the door. Leo and I both approached them as if we were part of the temple.

"Have you two found the mortals yet?" One of the dark robed men inquired.

I had my head bowed to obscure my face and whispered back, “No, nothing.” I saw the man open the temple door and he walked in with the other two. Leo and I both followed behind them. When we entered, I began looking around and there were paintings of dragons designed elaborately along the temple’s marble walls, all in an array of vibrant colors. The paintings told stories of each of the creatures’ lives. I could not understand the language that was written on the walls, so I followed the pictures. These dragons were protectors of different sacred objects in the world. It showed the red dragon protecting a chest. It appeared that this dragon lived next to a volcano. If only I knew were this volcano was on this island, I could find this creature.

These dragons were the colors of the elements they lived in. The red dragon was of fire dragon, the blue represented water, and there were also green and silver dragons as representatives of earth and air. Though they were not the only dragons, they were pictured as possessing sacred blessings by the Gods. The paintings and scripture were incredibly detailed. I was drawn into all the paintings and I could not believe how beautiful this place was. There were statues of dragons along the great hall, paintings along the wall, and enormous vases filled with flowers that were formed together to look like reptilian creatures. They had frankincense burning in each corner of the room. The walls were white marble and there were polished granite floors.

I followed the men down a long hallway of ornate art and rich incense until we arrived at a set of large, elaborately carved wooden doors. Two hooded men opened them while the others walked in. Leo and I both looked at each other and followed them. We came to a large chamber that looked like a king’s throne room. Monks gathered in the very center, forming a massive circle. They stood there with torches and were chanting the same phrase over and over. It was very relaxing to my ears and at the far end of the room was the leader. He sat on a throne, which was carved in the shape of a dragon. Its arms and legs ended in sharp claws and above the leader's head was the intimidating face of a dragon. It was beautifully designed out of wood, gold, and red velvet. I was suddenly distracted by a monk in front of us when he began to speak.

"We have searched many parts of the island and have found nothing of any mortal. Are you sure master, that there are mortals on this island?" The man asked, afraid of what the leader would say.

"Do not ever doubt me, Moore! I know there are mortals on this island and we will find them before dawn! Do you understand me!? The prophecy is about to take place. The planet Garis has almost lined up with Ark, northeast from the blazing golden sun within the center of our galaxy. The dual white dwarf sun orbits our planet, constantly along the horizon, but will soon be eclipsed by our moon Elijah, which will block out its light. Soon our world, Noven, along with Tabern, will be in the same direction of Garis and Ark. We will be directly behind them. Bane and the planet Xen will soon be east of the blazing sun. Their moons will be on the west. This will cause the planets Garis and Ark to block our view of the central sun. The gravity response will drag every planet in the same pattern infinitely!

"This will destroy seasons and years as we know them, leaving us with nothing but eternal darkness. When this happens, evil shall reign over the planet and the dark God, Sceptor, will rule this world and all of mankind shall fall to his whim. This leaves us no hope but to stop those that dare try to find Nebula. If Sceptor is resurrected with the power of the sword, the planets will stay aligned for eternity. We must make sure this doesn't happen. Now, find these mortals and bring them to me. I want them alive!" The leader commanded, holding his long golden staff, decorated with diamonds and a large crystal at the top. The man in front of me turned to face me, then walked past Leo and I as we continued to stand there in front of the leader.

"What is it you two want?" He asked with his strong and powerful voice. "Did you both not hear what I said earlier to the man in front of you? Now go and find these mortals!" he demanded, now angrier than the first time. Leo and I both looked at each other. I then turned to the door and was about to leave, when I thought I heard the leader's voice bellow across the room. "Kain! That is Kain! Grab them both quickly!"

I turned and saw that the leader was now standing with his staff. An army of men charged after Leo and I. When I turned back to leave through the doors, I noticed they had been shut and locked. The men grabbed us both. I could hear Leo yelling my name and saw him being taken away.

"Leo! Let him go, you fools!" I screamed, throwing monks left and right. I fought with incredible strength, but there were still too many monks to fight off. I felt myself falling to the ground; I was being beaten by staffs and drugged by darts. There was no way I could get up and I felt myself falling into a deep, dark sleep.

I had awoken in a dungeon filled with rats and filthy hay. The simple act of lying on the straw made me ill by just thinking about what crawled through it. I got up and walked over to the metal bars that caged me in this pile of filth. I peered ahead of me to see what was beyond the dreadful cell. As my eyes adjusted to the darkness, I saw the long, murky hallway ahead of the cell, built and floored in rough stone. This was absolutely sickening, compared to the beauty of the remainder of the temple. It smelled like death. Rats gnawed on the flesh of a corpse in the corner of the cell that only the Gods only knew how long it had been there. I began to wonder how I was going to get the hell out of there when I heard voices and footsteps. Three black robed men walked behind the leader, approaching me. The towering wig on the master brushed the top of the dungeon ceiling, collecting an unimaginable degree of grime. He came up to me with his regal staff and he began to speak.

"Well, well, well... what do we have here?" He said, placing the top of his staff under my chin and lifting my head. I looked at him with his dragon headed mask on.

"Why don't you show your face? Perhaps you fear to let me see your true form?" I replied, looking quite devilish with my eyes. I was strong and powerful. He knew it as well. I could have bent these bars or destroyed this filthy place with a blink of my eye if I desired it, but that was not the time.

"You think I fear you? Ha ha ha! I fear no one, mortal! It is you who will destroy us all and I will not allow it! The prophecy has begun and it is all your fault. You work for the vile God, Sceptor. I shall not allow you to leave this island alive!" He declared. I just stared at him with eyes full of hate.

"Where is Leo? He had better be alright or I will rip open your flesh and tear your filthy heart from your chest! I can destroy you and I will, for you're just a moronic fool to me! Now, let me out of here and let me continue my work," I demanded, hearing him laugh now even louder than before.

"Oh what a character you are! You dare challenge me, mortal!? I am the God Isaiah! I can crush your pathetic bones into paste! Rip out your intestines and choke you with them! How dare you mortal, to think you can destroy me!" He shouted with barbaric laughter in his voice. He was a monstrous being and the Gods only know what he looked like. He was making me sick. I then clapped my hands as if applaud his foolish outburst.

"Bravo, at least you keep me entertained, but that's all you are: a show." I said with a grin, folding my arms and watching his every move. I saw his eyelids lower over his eyes halfway. He was enraged and I knew he wanted to kill me right then and there.

"So... you think yourself better? You will be sacrificed to the fire dragon by dawn. If you survive, it will be a blessing from the God of light. I will not allow you to get away and by the moon and the stars, you will perish in hands of the fire dragon!" He bellowed, turning his back on me and walking back to the end of the hallway as three robed men followed him. I saw a large door at the end open and shut, then lock behind it. I wish I knew were Leo was and I hoped he was alright. I thought this would be a great time to escape, when I heard voices off by the door.

"I have captured one of the mortals' creatures. I will lock it up with the other," one of the men said behind the door. I tried to think what creature that was and I remembered that Franchesca was out waiting for us. I then heard the door open and the man along with Franchesca walked in. They both came up to me and the bars were opened. I looked at Franchesca, who was bound with a chain.

"Pssst... It's me, Kain," the robed man whispered. The man removed the hood. To my shock, I gazed upon the face of Tobit.

"Tobit!" I shouted in surprise.

"Shh... be quiet. This ain't the first time I've had to bust a friend out of a dungeon. I know what I'm doing," He said quietly. He then took my hand. "Come on, let's get the hell out of rat infested hole." He led me to the door and whispered, "Stay here Kain." He opened it with Franchesca by our side. As soon as we stepped to the next room, Tobit quickly grabbed the hooded man that stood guarding the dungeon entrance. He stuck his sword in the back of the robed man and slid him into the dungeon area. I then took the robe off the man and put it on. Tobit and I shut the door and walked out. Franchesca followed behind us.

"I know where they're keeping your man. Let's go bust him out." He said, waving his hand. I followed him and he guided us to another door. A man stood there in a black robe with a spear.

"Where do you think you're going?" the man said, holding the spear up to Tobit.

"Well, we have one of the mortal's creatures. We wish to lock it up until dawn," Tobit replied with his head lowered and the hood covering his face.

"Alright, do as you wish. They will be sacrificed to the fire dragon at dawn," The man exclaimed, then whispered to himself, "Who has a pet panther?" He shrugged and went back to his duties.

We chuckled and walked through the door that connected to a second dungeon. In the distance, I could see where Leo was being held captive. He sat in the corner of a dark, filthy cell with his knees bent close to his chest. Relieved to find him at last, I ran up to where he was trapped, my face still covered by my hood.

"Oh, great! They got Franchesca too! Damn it! Where is Kain, you monsters?!" Leo growled as we approached. He was going mad and began grabbing the bars. I then took my hood off and grinned at him with my light, pale blue eyes. I saw Leo's face soften, despite the shock.

"My prince? How did you get out? And-" He stammered, coming to his feet.

"Shhhh... Leo, it's okay, Tobit and Franchesca helped me get out," I said quietly to him. Tobit took off his hood and smiled with the old, rusty, keys dangling in his fingers. Tobit slid the key in the hole and I grabbed Leo out of the dirty stone cell. "Come on Leo, let's get out of here!" I exclaimed. I walked up to the door beyond which the man stood guard with his robe. I grabbed him, cracked his neck quickly, and took off his robe. I slid the dead monk in the dungeon and gave the robe to Leo.

"Here, put this on," I said to Leo with a grin. Leo put the robe on and we briskly walked out of the dungeon, shutting the door behind us. Tobit took my hand and led us through the hall over to a large black door. It was beautifully carved in relief with images of dragons. Opening it only a crack, we squinted our eyes to see a grand hall filled with robed men and the eerie sound of chanting. This was the side of the leader's room, where we were caught before. The leader was speaking in another language and the monks stood and chanted with torches in their hands. What in the name of the Gods were they doing? Isaiah began to speak in our language.

"By dawn, the mortals will be sacrificed to the fire dragon and the prophecy will no longer continue. Our world will be saved and we can all live by the God of light," He declared. I was watching this in the shadow behind the cracked door, along with Tobit and Leo. Franchesca could not see anything behind us, but listened with her keen panther ears. The leader finished his speech and slowly walked over to the main entrance and two monks opened the way for him. The leader walked beyond and all the monks followed him in a line. I waited for them to leave before speaking.

"The way out is through that door, right?" I asked Tobit. He nodded his head and we quietly walked over to the door that Isaiah walked through. After that, all we had to do was walk down that hall with the paintings and leave through the main door and we would be free. When we approached the exit, we slowly opened it and noticed the monks were gone. *Where did they go?* An eerie silence permeated as we strode through the door. We then quickly, but quietly ran down the hall and exited through the main entrance. I began to laugh insanely to myself while Leo and Franchesca gawked at me.

"What in the name of Vertigo is wrong with you? Are you crazy or something? You always seem to think things are funny right when we are in the middle of danger!" Tobit exclaimed to me as we ran over to a line of bushes. I continued to laugh more, but covering my mouth so I did not cackle loudly enough for us to be heard. I followed Tobit and hid beneath the brush. I felt filthy and I wished I was home bathing with flowers and scented oils. I found myself daydreaming of this to the point where Tobit slapped me across the face! I held my aching cheek in shock, releasing a feminine cry.

"Wake up you fool! Now what do we do, oh great prince of danger?" Tobit asked me with a hint of sarcasm in his voice.

"Stop worrying, my friend. We will get the map and escape this island, trust me," I replied with a chuckle. Leo shook his head and looked at Franchesca, who returned his gaze and smiled with her panther eyes. I was excited at the thought of what could happen to us next. I had an insatiable taste for danger that only just began to grow within me. I was starving for it and everyone knew it. As I contemplated this, I looked around and noticed that weariness had taken hold on our friends; none of us were rested. I was lost in deep thought when I felt Leo pull on my sleeve.

"Kain, is there a way for us to perhaps get some sleep; poor Tobit has not rested in days," Leo said to me so softly with his sad, handsome eyes.

"Leo, Leo, Leo, how adorable of you. Yes, it would be wonderful to get some sleep, but how can we with these monks after us? What if they find us?" I asked, touching Leo's hair. He looked back at me with that same cute, handsome face.

"Great, not even Mr. Chuckles and Giggles can get us out of this one. So, does anyone have any brilliant, not so dangerous ideas?" Tobit asked, rubbing his eyes and head. I knew he did not mean his sarcasm from the exhaustion, but in a way, I enjoyed it. I actually thought it quite funny. I began laughing and poor Tobit grew even angrier.

"Why is it you laugh at everything? Do you not understand that there are people out there trying to kill us? For the Gods' sake man, we are to be sacrificed to a fire dragon! How thick can you get? Is it that you cannot see our flesh being burnt and our bones turning to ashes? Or could it be that you think that you, with your powers and gifts from your dark God, will save you? The Gods only know that you are probably just some monster disguised as an angel! Man, this ain't worth a sack of gold! I must have lost my mind to follow you fools into this death trap." Tobit was rambling, nearly screaming at the same time. I had to grab him and pull him close to me in order to snap him out of it. I wrapped my arms around him and hugged him.

I then whispered into his ear, "Please be quiet, my friend, we will get through this. I am no monster and I will prove that to you soon. Please stop, I know you're tired and that all you need is rest. I appreciate your wonderful help. You're a good man Tobit, and you will be known as a hero someday. Trust me." I rubbed his back softly and I felt him hug me back.

"I'm sorry, it's just... you're right. I'm tired and perhaps even scared, frightened of what might happen to us. All this talk of the prophecy and the Gods is too much for me to handle. I am no warrior. In the name of Vertigo, I am a simple sailor, a captain of a small ship." He said to me, at last calmer than before.

"Right, I say we get some sleep soon," I exclaimed. I rose to my feet and began trying to find a place where we can hide and rest for a bit. I walked on my own to search for a while, and when I thought I found a suitable place, I heard footprints. Was it Leo, Tobit, or Franchesca? I looked behind me and when I turned back, there was the silhouette of a stranger standing in front of me. I grinned at him and pulled out my sword. He was fast and began throwing me down to the ground. I was shocked at his strength. I then got back up with ease... he let me. *Was he playing games with me? Who was this man?* I charged at him with all my power and swung my sword for his head. He blocked my swing with his sword. All that could be heard in the night was the clashing of metal and dirt being kicked. I thought of using my power. I created a ball of fire in my hand and threw it at him with all my strength. The ball then flew towards him and before hitting him, turned to ice and fell before him. My eyes were wide open and I was shocked at what I just saw.

"What the hell!" I shouted, looking at the shattered ice at his feet, "Who are you?!" The man ran up to me with his sword and began fighting me again. My strength was not as powerful as his. Perhaps this was the leader and he really meant what he said in the temple. I was pushed to the ground with immense force. He landed on top of me and I blocked his sword with mine as he pushed down on my blade. I was on my back, looking up at him. I tried to see his face under the hood, but it was obscured in shadow. I heard his voice and it was eerily familiar, a very soothing tone. *Who was this man?*

"Well, well, well, seems you have turned your back on your destiny, dear boy..." The man said, "You should not even have such a gift of power if you do not use it to complete your fate. And so it seems you learned how to use it for the opposite purpose... ironic. Who taught you? I should destroy you right now, but it seems that I must finish what you started. You were a good little boy, why couldn't you just have stayed that way forever? Now you hunger for love and peace! You have forgotten about power and you even dare try to destroy me!" He removed his hood and I almost fainted at the sight.

"Mas…ter?" I stammered, shocked and lost in him. I looked at his hair and face. "Dear Gods, is it really you?" I asked, staring at him. He looked back at me fiercely and grinned. I then turned my head and heard approaching footsteps.

I looked back at Ariaus and heard him say, "Well, I have no time for you boy, see you around…" he then leapt off me and ran into the forest. I was still shocked that it was him and could not even get up. I looked above to see monks circling me and shook my head, trying to get up. I screamed for Leo and Tobit, but they were already caught along with Franchesca, bound together in chains.

"No! Let me go!" I screamed. *My master cannot get that map before us!* I thought helplessly. I was not going to allow this. "Let me go! You are going to allow evil to get the map! You have the wrong person!" I shrieked. They ignored my pleas, shot me with darts, and beat me with their staves. I was getting weak and tired. I then said, growing dizzy and feeling the drug flow through me, “No... master...”

Chapter Nine
Sacrificed

I awoke back in the dungeon, but this time I was chained to the wall. I looked to the side of me and I saw Leo and Tobit were chained as well. I then looked down below them and Franchesca's paws were chained so she could not run off. I saw some light from a small window and I knew it had to be morning. As the monks gathered about the dungeon, I knew I had failed. The leader walked up to me.

"Well, I see you are awake, Dark Prince. Are you ready to be sacrificed to the fire dragon?" He said laughing, and touching my face through the bars. I was so weak and tired that I could not even look at him in the face. I tried to find the strength to tell him about Ariaus, but I could not form the sounds from my throat.

The leader then turned his back and was about to leave when I yelled out to him, "Wait! There is someone else on this island... you cannot do this to me! You have the wrong man, my master is here and he will get the map! He is the one who works for the dark God, not me! Please do not do this to us... please..." I begged him. He looked at me oddly and walked up to me. He then stared at me, touching my hair at the same time.

"What is this nonsense you speak, boy?" he asked, trying to read my mind. I gazed at him with my sad eyes.

"Please believe me,"I whispered to him.

"My Gods, are you that much of a warlock that you even have the gift to make me believe the lies you create. Even when I read your mind, it shows these lies," He said, still staring at me oddly.

"That's because they are not lies!" I exclaimed.

"You are a character, dark prince. It is unfortunate that it is you that we must destroy. You are quite amusing; you would be wonderful to have around. Sadly, that isn't going to be so," He said, laughing charmingly to himself.

He was still wearing the mask and robe, but I wanted to see what he looked like underneath. I then saw the leader walk away from me and over twelve monks came up to me and took me out of the chains. They then tied my hands behind my back and they did the same to Leo and Tobit. Franchesca wore a chain around her neck as they took us out of the temple. We began a long walk through pathways in the woods that grew harder to walk on as we tread through them. We were climbing upwards for hours and as we reached the top, the temperature steadily rose. When we arrived at the Summit, there was a large cave and lava where bright orange magma poured out from small cracks in the ground. I could not believe this was where they would keep a paper map. I then felt the monks drag me over to a large wooden post. There was a ladder against it which they used to drag me upward. I was tied to it by my hands and feet. My hands were behind my back. I could not believe this is how they sacrifice people.

"So where is the dragon?" I asked one of the monks. He then pointed in the direction of the cave. I looked at it and saw smoke begin to spew out of it. "Great!" I said to myself. I saw Leo, Tobit and Franchesca on the ground. Leo's eyes were red from tears. I felt terrible; I did not want him to cry. I looked at him sadly, then Tobit and Franchesca. I wanted to tell Leo not to cry when I thought of telling him telepathically. *Do not cry, Leo. Everything will be all right*. I tried telling him. I then saw him look up at me oddly; maybe he heard it. I smiled down to him. Thc monks began to play their drums in tune with the rhythm of my heartbeat. I stared at the cave and saw a large, shiny and red, glasslike head pop out of the cave.

I could not believe how beautiful this dragon looked. It appeared exactly like stained red glass. I saw the way the sun shined down on this dragon and how I could nearly see through him. What was this creature? My Gods, it looked like a type of sculpture. I was shocked and could not understand the glossy body of this enormous dragon. I then looked down. To my surprise, I spied Leo trying to fight off the monks.

"Kain!" He shouted. He was going insane and there was nothing I could do. I looked back at the dragon and saw his entire body. This creature was so massive that he appeared larger than the volcano itself. Steam rose up from the ground and from the dragon's nose and mouth. The dragon flew straight up to me and I heard it speak. It spoke, but I did not see its mouth move! I then plead to it telepathically.

Fire dragon, you cannot do this! I work for the God of light, you must believe me. There is another one who is after this map who is working for the dark God, Sceptor. You cannot allow it! Please listen to me! I sent my thoughts to him with my eyes closed. I hoped that the dragon could read my thoughts. I was waiting for him to say something.

"So, you are the dark prince? I shall not listen to your pathetic begging," The dragon exclaimed in a deep, booming voice. He walked closer to me so that I could feel the steam of his hot breath from his nose and mouth. I was burning up with heat and already I thought that my life was over.

Please dragon, you must believe me! I said in my thoughts. I felt there was no hope and I yelled out, "Vertigo, save me! How can you allow this!? The world will be over!" I then stared at the dragon as tears fell from my eyes. The dragon stared at me and then at the monks and my friends.

"You really mean what you say, don't you, dark prince?" It asked with amusement. I shook my head up and down. The dragon looked at the monks and bared his teeth. They feared the dragon and begged him not to hurt them. The leader stood steadfast with his staff, yet he trembled; he knew what the dragon was thinking. The beast let out a loud cry that nearly awakened the volcano. I saw the dragon's large finger with a nail the size of my sword cut the rope from my hands and feet. I was then clutched in his hand and placed gently down on the ground. The dragon's wings were flapping back and forth.

Causing a large wind, he began to speak to me again. "I know now that you need this map and why. Here, follow me." The monks stood there with their torches as I walked up to Leo. I looked at the monks that held him one by one, along with Tobit and Franchesca.

"Let them go, now!" I demanded. The monks looked at the leader with confusion and he nodded his head. The monks untied my friends and let us follow the dragon. I heard the leader mumble to his head monk, Moore.

"I do not understand, the prophecy says that only one who holds true love may take the map from the fire dragon. How can this man, who was chosen by the dark God, be able to take this map with the dragon's permission?" He asked. I followed the dragon into the cave and everyone followed behind me, except for the monks and the leader. We walked past bones and skulls from others who had tried to get the map with no avail. When we reached the belly of the cave, there was a fire burning in the middle, and inside this flame was the chest. This flame burned eternally without harming the object in the center. The dragon stared at the flame and as his eyes locked on, the fire disappeared.

The chest could now be opened, but the surface was still too hot for a human to touch. I pulled out the key to the chest and knelt beside it. I placed it in the keyhole and turned it carefully. The lid to the golden chest opened and a map lay in the blue velvet lining. I looked at the dragon and mentally asked him if I could take it from the chest. The dragon nodded and I slowly tried to put my hand in the chest without touching the sides; if my skin made contact with them, I would run the risk of terrible burns. I took the map and key out slowly and moved away from the chest, which then closed on its own and the flame covered it again.

This part of the cave was vast and there were crystals growing outside of the stone walls. This place shimmered and there was a hole at the top of the cave where light shined in on this chest from above, just like in the tower that Franchesca was cursed to protect. I looked at the map and saw that it was drawn out with complete detail. There were drawings of unicorns and dragons of all colors surrounding the page. It was beautiful and it showed directly where to go next. It would be a long journey ahead of us. Before I could figure out where to go next, there was a loud cracking sound. I then felt the ground beneath me shake and I saw lava pouring out only feet away from me. I could not believe what was happening. I looked at the fire dragon and then peered at my friends.

"What is going on?" I shouted in fear.

"Do not be afraid, but we must get out of here fast!" The dragon replied. His voice was deep and rumbled the ground just as the lava did.

"This volcano is going to explode!" Leo exclaimed. I grabbed his hand and guided him out to the cave. Tobit and Franchesca followed us along with the dragon. I came out to see the monks staring at us. As soon as the magma caught their eye, they fled alongside us. The dragon grabbed the back of my shirt and lifted me up along with Leo, who dangled from my hand.

"Dear Gods! What are you doing?" I yelled out. The dragon placed me on his back with Leo following in tow. The dragon then picked up Tobit, followed by Franchesca, who ran into the palm of his hand. Once we had settled upon the creature's back, he spread his wings and, with a heavy push from his massive legs, he took off into the air. As he soared high into the sky, I could see the monks and the leader staring up at us. My eyes widened in amazement as they continued to run for their lives. I began to laugh and I looked over at Leo. I then laughed louder and the dragon did as well. When we reached the end of the island, I spied a ship in the distance. As I strained my eyes to see, I observed that this was not Tobit's vessel. I did not know whose ship that was until I spied the black flag of the kingdom of Tarot and realized that it belonged to my master.

"Hey! Whose ship is that next to mine?" Inquired Tobit.

"I believe it's my master's ship. I saw him on the island. He tried to get to the map before me. He wants the sword so he can continue the prophecy on behalf of the dark god, Sceptor. It is I who must stop his madness before this so-called prophecy does take place." I said, holding onto the dragon.

"So where do we go now, prince of fools?" Tobit asked. I looked at him and laughed in his face.

"Tobit, Tobit, Tobit... how I love your sarcasm." I replied, turning forward to see where the dragon was taking us.

"Why does he laugh? Does he think of me as a fool?" Tobit whispered to Leo.

"That is just the way Kain is, he laughs at everything and it's very hard to hurt him," Leo responded. I snickered to myself and shook my head. Tobit put his head on Leo's shoulder and within minutes, fell asleep. I looked at the map and could not help but think about our next move.

"So, let's figure out where the next destination points us to. This map is a full illustration of our world, Noven." I mentioned to my crew. I looked closer, trying to find what made this map worth all the effort. To me, it resembled any normal chart I had ever seen with no special distinction. There were no magic letters appearing on the page, no markings of unknown lands and castles, and worst of all, no mention of the lost sword, Nebula. I clenched my teeth in frustration; people died to protect this measly roll of parchment.

"Nothing... this map is useless," I whispered to myself. In the rush of winds, nobody else heard me. I shook my head and strained my eyes to spot any detail out of the ordinary, but saw nothing.

"Kain, look!" Leo shouted, shaking me from my thoughts. I turned my head to face him with a confused expression. "Your pouch... it's glowing!" I looked down at where my coin purse hung from my belt. To my shock, it radiated with brilliant light. I opened the clasp and dug into it, grasping the compass key I had stored inside. Pulling it out, I gazed at the object in shock. It shone with brightness that illuminated the dusky sky before me. Everyone turned their heads in my direction, wide-eyed and astonished by what they saw.

My hands shaking, I hovered the key over the map. *Could it be that these two sacred objects work together?* I thought to myself. All of a sudden, my vision flashed white; my friends and the evening sky disappeared. Blurred images entered my head of a forest filled with fireflies that illuminated in blue, trees that were not natural, but transparent and gleaming as if made of glass. With a whoosh, my consciousness passed by with impossible speed. The forest cleared and in my line of vision was an enormous tower made of iridescent crystal that shone with the light of the stars.

I knew then that was where we needed to head next. My mind and body felt desperately hell-bent on reaching that place. *That must be it,* I thought. *Perhaps that is where the blade is being kept.* As soon as the vision flashed into my mind, it disappeared, fading back to the moonlit sky. Night had fallen and my companions were staring at me.

"Kain! Kain! Are you alright? What happened to you?" Shouted Leo.

"I know where to go!" I exclaimed. "The map showed me a vision of a tower made of crystal. Let's go, my friends!" I reached my arm up with joy. "Dragon, have you ever heard of this place?"

"I have, but I do not know where it resides. Just tell me where on the map to go and I shall take you there." The dragon replied with a powerful voice.

"Well, the map does not say how to get there. All I got was a vision somewhere in a crystal forest. Maybe you know of that location?" I asked the dragon.

"Sadly I do not, but I do know of a village nearby that would know more about the tower; the people who live there are experts on what lies hidden in the world of Noven. This place you speak of may not even be of this realm. By the way, my name is Raphael. I am one of the seven Dragons who stand ever ready to enter the presence of the glory of Vertigo. I was chosen by the God of light to protect the map from evil." He responded.

What an amazing dragon he was, his skin was pearly and translucent, appearing to be made of red crystal. The sun shined through him and off of him, creating a rainbow effect against the misty sky. Raphael continued to fly over the sparkling sea. I spied the coast in the distance, which was littered with small settlements.

"I shall land at that tiny village below," Raphael said, pointing to a cluster of straw buildings on the shore. I nodded in agreement. We did need information on how to get to this Tower of Crystal. As soon as we drew close, Raphael made his descent. As we approached, the settlement appeared misty and abandoned. When I jumped off of Raphael, I began yelling out loud,

"Hello? Is there anyone here?" I asked. I waited for someone to pop out. At that moment, a small dwarf sprang out from behind a tree. He had a fierce expression on his face and aimed his bow and arrow in our direction.

"Be gone from our home, monsters! We do not allow humans or dragons on our village! Now leave us in peace! You tall mortals have stolen nearly all our land! At least allow us to keep this. Now, be gone!" He exclaimed. I began to laugh at him, how rude I must have sounded, but I was unable to help myself.

"I am sorry, dear friend. We are not here for your land, but rather, for your knowledge. If you can just tell us where we could find the Tower of Crystal, then I would be most happy to leave you and your village in peace," I explained kindly. He then stared at me, thinking of whether or not he should tell us. Judging by his upright posture and garb, he was the leader of the township. In spite of his courage and authority, I felt bad for the people he governed. What king would do this to these innocent people?

"All right! I will tell you," The man said with a sigh, walking over to me. He then stopped as a rumbling sound could be heard in the distance. "Riders! Everyone quickly, run and hide!" the man shouted in fear. He stared at us briefly, and then quickly began leading children with their parents into the safety of their homes. I looked around to see what this man was yelling about. When I looked behind Raphael , I spotted at least twenty men on horses charging toward the village. With haste, I unsheathed my sword and Leo did the same and ran toward me. Tobit woke with a start as Franchesca jumped off of Raphael's back.

I waited, standing patiently still, for the men on horses to charge into range. Leo and I were both back to back, grasping our swords at the ready. One of the riders rode past me and I did not hesitate to slice his belly open. His intestines fell out as he tumbled off his horse. Raphael then let out a large, monstrous cry and launched an enormous ball of fire from his snout. The flame hit the two men off their horses. The man next to them shrieked in fear as he bucked his horse and led it in the opposite direction. Unfortunately, two more charged forward and slammed spiked maces into Raphael's wings, causing him to roar in pain.

I dropped my sword and stared at the riders as they began to slaughter the villagers in their homes. I closed my eyes and concentrated on a black dragon with a sharp tail, deadly fangs, and ghastly pointed claws. As I concentrated, a black cloud of smoke billowed from around me. The surrounding air became chilled as the form of a dragon rose from the dark mist. I was frozen in my power, yet I knew I could control the creature. When I spoke, the black dragon moved its scaly lips with mine.

"FOOLS! Leave this place or you shall feel my wrath!" The dragon bellowed my words with a booming voice. I willed the beast to open its mouth and launch balls of fire and daggers of ice into the flesh of the invaders. The Riders collapsed to the ground from left to right. The ones that still stood grew frightened and ran off. My silhouette shone from the black mist and my eyes glowed in icy purple. Leo even fell back from me and stared at me from the ground. I turned my head to see that there were no more men attacking the village. I used my black dragon to pick up the dead bodies of the men and place them back on their horses. I had my dragon cry with a piercing voice and scared all the horses out of the village, then concentrated on making the dragon disappear back into a cloud of fog. When the image dissipated, I opened my eyes and noticed the villagers gawking at me. Raphael turned to me in disbelief. Even I was shocked. I looked at Leo on the ground and laughed a bit. I felt myself growing very weak. I fell to the dirt and closed my eyes.

I awoke in a very small house, more cramped than the old woman's in the forest. A small woman came up to me and placed a cold cloth on my forehead. I blinked at her and struggled to speak, "Thank you very much, dear." The woman smiled at me and handed me a cup filled with hot tea.

"Your friends are outside. The chief wishes to speak with you when you feel better," the woman said kindly. I then got up from the small bed and bent to walk out of the tiny door. After exiting, I lifted my eyes to see a large crowd of people. Leo, Franchesca, Tobit, and Raphael were all surrounded by the tiny villagers. The chief congratulated them while providing directions to where to find the Tower of Crystal. *Figures, I miss this!* I thought. I walked over to the crowd and everyone looked at me. What did they think of me? I tried to read their thoughts and by doing so, I heard what each one of them was thinking. Many of them revered me as powerful and others thought of me as demonic. Some even saw me as a blessing from the Gods. Nevertheless, they still feared me. I looked at them with my dark eyes and hair completely a mess. I grinned down at the small men and women, who stood at my waist in height. The chief looked at me with fearful, but thankful eyes.

"Now, I wish to know where this Tower of Crystal is. Will you tell me?" I asked with the most charming voice. I folded my arms and stared at the small man, who continued to stare up at me. He climbed up on a table and handed me a ring with a large white crystal in it. The stone was beautiful and I could have stared at it for hours. I looked at the small man on the table.

"This ring is a gift to you and your friends. This is our way of thanking you. The ring has a magical ability to it. It will glow brighter when you get closer to the Tower. That crystal is from the structure itself. It shall guide you straight in its direction. Now please stay and feast with us tonight. By the way, my name is Roland. I am the chief of this clan," He said, bowing to me.

I then smiled at him charmingly, slipped the ring on my index finger, and whispered, "My name is Prince Kain and these are my friends, Sir Leo, Tobit, Franchesca and the dragon of protection, Raphael." All of a sudden, I remembered that I have not seen Gordock in some time. "Where is Gordock?" I asked. I looked around and still could not find him. "When was the last time we saw him?" I asked again, getting worried. "Great, I lost him back at the island." I looked up into the sky and then began yelling for him. The villagers were looking around and then at me as if I was crazy. "Gordock! Where are you, Gordock?!" I yelled.

No one knew where he went or where he could be or even, for that matter, what he *was,* as I had no time to explain that he was in fact a raven. I sighed, hoping that he would show up. What would the old woman think of me now? I bowed my head, looking at the ring. It was silver and shined with the reflection of the sun. I looked at Roland and smiled. "Well, thank you very much for your help. I do believe we will be staying with you to feast and perhaps if you do not mind, rest?" I asked. Roland smiled at me and then laughed softly to himself.

"Of course you can stay the night. Your friends look weak and tired. I would only be rude to not allow all of you to stay the night. Raphael, I will have my finest healers tend to your wounds. It will be a while before you can fly again," He exclaimed with a soothing voice. I smiled at him and then at Leo. Leo looked at me as if I was crazy and I just patted his back. I kissed his cheek quickly before anyone noticed and walked over to lean against a tree by myself. I pulled out my father's letter that I told myself that I would read once I got on the ship. I gingerly put the pieces back together and began reading.

Dear Kain,

I wish I could see you before I go. By now I am sure you know of what the illness has done to me. I love you, my son. Someday, we will be together and the Gods will allow me to see you once again. I wish I could have saved you from that monster who took you and killed your mother. I want you to know the one who killed your mother. His name was Ariaus, he one who now calls himself your master. He murdered her before taking you from me. You cannot allow him to control you, nor make you work for Sceptor. You must realize something, that love is greater than power. If you fall into the hands of Sceptor, then the world is damned in darkness. If you break the link between you and him, then you can save this world from Sceptor's dark hand. Now I know how you hate to be told what to do, but for once listen to what I have to say, my son. Your brother loves you, all you have to do is love him back. I love you. May Vertigo shine his light within you. I will be watching and guiding you...

Sincerely,
Your Father
Autumn 2, 44562 YoN

I began to cry and crinkled up the letter. I was lost and I did not want him to stop writing. I wish he was here. "Father, I am sorry..." I sobbed to myself. "I love you, father... why did you have to die? *Why*?" The tears dripped down my face. *I must do this for him, I must get through this and I will protect my brother. I must not allow Sceptor to control me.* I thought. I wiped the tears off my face and walked over to Leo, who was talking to Roland. I took his hand and whispered to him, "Please come with me." I looked at Roland and said, "Please excuse us for a moment." I took Leo to a line of trees out of the village and hid us behind a trunk. I looked at him, leaning my back against the bark and pulled him close to me. A tear then dropped down from my eye and I saw his smile turn into a frown.

"Kain, what is wrong, my sweet?" he asked tenderly, wiping the tear away. "Why is it you cry?" I stared at him, slowly moved close to his lips, and kissed him. I wrapped my arms around his back and held him. I began crying on his shoulder and I needed him to be with me. I was devastated and I knew that if he was there, I would get over it faster.

I begged, "I love you Leo, please do not leave me..." I kissed his ear and his cheek, then held him tighter.

Leo wrapped his arms around me and whispered, "Kain, I will never leave you. I love you. I will be here for you as long as you wish." I wanted to cry even more when he said that. We held each other for some time and I told him everything about what my father wrote and how I felt. The hours were going by fast and I decided now that it will be time to eat soon. I could smell food cooking over a large fire and music began to play. Leo and I both moved from our spot and began walking over to the feast. When Leo and I both walked to the center of the small village, they clapped and smiled at us. I smiled back and began laughing softly. I saw Raphael lying down next to the fire with Franchesca on his back. Tobit was on the ground, eating a large piece of meat. It looked delicious and I saw they had wine as well. The villagers were singing and dancing as we walked closer to the fire. Roland then stood up from the hearth and greeted us with meat on a bone and a cup of wine. I laughed charmingly and began feasting on the delicious food. We drank and sang for hours. The time flew as we danced with the villagers and enjoyed the beautiful night sky. The villagers put on a show for us and they were hilarious and wonderful to watch. I could have stayed there forever in that moment.

When the night grew late and villagers were getting weary, I thought it would be a great time to sleep. I walked over to Roland. "*Helluuu*... my *companions* an' I would luv' t'get some *rest* now. *Is* that alright w'*chu*?" I asked tipsily, stumbling, and swaying still with the taste of wine upon my lips. My words slurred, vision blurred and my cheeks were slightly flushed.

He smiled and said, "Of course, I will take you to your beds." He then walked us over to a small house, where there were three beds, Leo and I along with Tobit followed him. It was very kind of them to do this for us. I thanked Roland kindly and lay down on the bed. Leo then lay next to me on my bed and smiled while Tobit shook his head, lying on his bed across the room. I laughed softly, covering my mouth so Tobit could not hear me. Leo laughed with me and held me. I held him tight and covered us with a warm blanket. I began to think of my father and what he said. I drifted in and out of sleep. My mind could not rest, though I was very tired. So very... tired...

Chapter Ten
Women Warriors

I awoke with Leo almost on top of me with his moist drool on my shirt. I raised my eyebrow and whispered to myself, “How disgusting...” I moved a bit to get up, but Leo was still on top of me and he was too heavy to move.

“Leo, love, please get up for a minute,” I said quietly in his ear. He moaned a bit, which I liked. “Hey, handsome? Are you going to move a bit for me?” I asked softly against his cheek. He then looked down at me under him. “Glad you’re awake, adorable one,” I said, wiping his drool off of me. I looked at him and he looked back at me with a smile. His hair was messy and his eyes were half open. “Aww...” I said, sliding my fingers through his hair. I then looked to see if Tobit was awake. Surprisingly he was not, so I kissed Leo on his cheek and then slowly to his lips.

I loved kissing him softly. I felt Leo’s lips opening to mine, but I had to push him away from me. I did not want Tobit to wake up and see us. I smiled at him and whispered, “Leo, we cannot kiss that way! Tobit might wake up and see us,” I moved him a bit so I could sit up on the bed, when I felt his large hand grab my arm. I looked at him with soft, shocked eyes. “Leo? What are you do-” he stopped me with his lips on mine.

I felt his tongue slide in my mouth and he was kissing me passionately. I moaned a bit and I heard Tobit move. I moaned one more time, pushing him away. “Leo, stop!” I said, staring at him. He laughed softly to himself. What a stubborn fool! I knew now that Tobit was up, but pretending to be asleep. I then moved to stand up when I felt his hand grab me again.

“Leo... what are you doing?!” I snapped, trying to get away from him. He was laughing and then threw me on my back. I was now lying down on the bed again and he was completely on top of me, holding me down. “Leo!” I yelled as he continued to laugh then kiss my neck. “Stop it, you fool! Not now!” I did not mind what he did, but he was doing this at the wrong time. He thought of it as a joke. I was melting and could not stop him. I looked over at Tobit, who was looking at us. “Great! Leo, get up!” I said, slapping him on his chest. He laughed louder and now kissed me on my lips. I heard him moan, then for some odd reason it was like he was lifted off of me. I opened my eyes and saw Leo on the floor with Tobit standing there looking at him. I sat up and stared at Leo. Tobit looked down at me and whispered, “Are you okay, Kain?” I looked at him and then at Leo on the floor who was shocked. I then started to laugh and fell on my back. I laid there laughing and looked at Tobit.

“What is going on? Was he hurting you, Kain?” he asked with such a serious voice that I laughed louder. Leo began to laugh along with me. Poor Tobit stood there, shaking his head and folding his arms.

“I have had it with your laughter. This goes to both of you!” Tobit said as he walked out of the room. Tobit was angry and I could feel it. I looked at the door and Leo did the same. “See what you did?” I said to Leo.

“I am sorry Kain, I did not know he would do that.” Leo said.

“I told you this was not the place... why can’t you just listen to me at times?” I said with an exasperated sigh, getting up out of the bed and kicking him softly as he sat on the floor.

“Get up you bloody numbskull!” I demanded. I shook my head and he laughed. I walked out of the tiny hut with my hair still loose. I looked for Tobit and noticed how the fog was thick. “Tobit!?” I yelled. I heard nothing but the birds fluttering from the trees. I walked over to where Raphael was still sleeping next to the rock fire. His wings were freshly bandaged, lined with healing herbs as Tobit sat, patting Francesca.

As I approached, he stopped and turned his back from me. I lowered my head and smiled, then quickly made a serious face. I stood next to him and whispered, "I am sorry for the way I acted, Tobit. It was thoughtful of you to do that to Leo for me. I mean, I know you did not know what he was doing or if I wanted him to. Please forgive me for laughing. Out of everyone I call a fool, at times the only fool is me. Are you going to hate Leo and me, then leave us? I hope you don't, I would miss you here." I said softly, waiting for him to answer.

"Why do you bother to talk to me? You know I mean nothing to you and the same with Leo. I mean nothing to him as well. You both are using me to get to the sword! You laugh at what I say to mock me! After all the help I gave you, all you do is laugh at me!? I've had enough of your foolishness and you and your lover can weep all you want. I am leaving you and Leo to do this on your own. I am going home!" He exclaimed, walking away from me.

I looked straight ahead, shocked at what happened. *Was he supposed to say that?* I ran after him and tapped him on his shoulder. "Wait, Tobit! Please don't go! I know I can be a bloody ass, forgive me! You are a wonderful friend, please believe me!" I pleaded. I looked at him sadly with my icy blue eyes, but he only stared at me. I saw him move his hand over to my face and he touched my cheek. He then moved my hair away from my eyes and slid it behind my ear.

"I don't know what it is about you, but you have a beauty in you that can draw any man to believe you and even love you," Tobit said softly to me. I felt him kiss my cheek. I closed my eyes and let him. I did not want him to leave.

"Please don't leave, my friend." I said softly back to him.

"I am sorry Kain, but this is goodbye. I will find my own way back home. Good luck on your journey." I gazed at him and struggled to not cry. If I only did not act like a fool, he would be staying with us. I watched as Tobit walked out of the village. I turned around to see Franchesca and Raphael looking at me. I turned my head down; I felt like an idiot. I ran out of the village and called for him, "Tobit, wait!" But I could not hear him nor see him. I tried to look for him, but the fog was too thick. "Damn it!" I cried. I slowly walked back to the village and looked sadly up at Raphael. "It's all my fault. Why do I have to laugh at everything? I will never laugh again," I said, sitting down on the ground. When I looked up, I noticed Leo was standing above me looking down into my bright blue eyes.

"It's not your fault, Kain, It was mine. I should have more respect for people. It was I who laughed as well. I should have never done that to you," he said, softly touching my hair and kneeling down next to me. "It was not your fault. He is gone now and we still have to move on. We are wasting time sitting here. Let's say goodbye to the villagers and head for that tower!" Hugging Leo, I stood and approached the chief's door to knock. He walked out and I told him that we were going to go on our way. I thanked him for everything. He gave us food for our journey and waved as we left the village.

For hours we walked through a large, insect infested swampland, guided by a string of light that illuminated from the silver ring Roland gave to us. It was a daunting journey with bloodsucking flies biting into our skin at every turn. Our boots were ankle-deep, in filthy stinking mud, pasted to our fine leather boots. *It's too bad Raphael is still injured, or we could just fly over all of this vomit-inducing swamp,* I thought. This was when I wished we had Mage as well, so that we could quickly ride with the wind and escape the swarm. On our way to a large field, I saw a figure standing in the middle of the pathway. I removed my sword from its sheath. I ordered everyone to stay behind. Leo had his sword out as well and stood in front of Franchesca. I walked up to the creature slowly covered in a fog.

"Who are you? We mean no harm, but if you cause us to hurt you, then we will have to do so." I shouted with purpose. It continued to stand still as I snuck closer. As I approached, I spotted a mane of shaggy long white hair. The face was old and the eyes dark. I then heard a raven's caw. I stopped for a second and yelled, "Gordock?" I walked closer until I saw it was the old woman from the forest.

"I see you were not expecting me, dear boy," she chuckled softly to herself.

"What in the name of Vertigo are you doing here? And how did you find Gordock? Did you tell my brother of Ariaus and what I am trying to do?" I asked curiously.

"Slow down, dear boy. Indeed I informed your brother about Ariaus, but he did not believe me," she explained. "He had made sure that his solders would not allow me back in the castle afterward. He also suspects that you are holding Leo captive. He is paranoid you are going to hurt him. Your brother sent out legions of his men to search for you and they have been trying to track you down. I on the other hand used Gordock to watch you. I can see through his eyes. I did this so I could determine when you needed help. Now, as for your brother again, he will not believe you until he sees the truth for himself. Your brother is after you along with his knights. I know you are wondering how I got here, well, just do not worry about that. What you do have to think about is that a large amount of women warriors patrol this place. They travel in great packs and they are extremely powerful. They should not be too far from this area. I must go and I will leave Gordock with you so I can watch and make sure you are all right. Good luck, dear boy. Vertigo is with you." She exclaimed as she slowly faded away into a cloud of fog. I quickly charged at her and tried to grab her, but she was gone.

"Wait! Don't go!" I yelled. I looked around and heard Gordock let out another hark as he flew upward and perched himself on the branch of an aged, wilted tree. I sighed and walked over to Leo. Raphael stood, his large clawed feet and his tail swung back and forth. Even in the dim gray fog, he was beautiful.

"Kain... how did that old woman get here? How can we trust her?" Leo inquired, carefully pushing his hair back away from his eyes.

I helped him and whispered, "I do not know my friend, I do not know. Let's continue our journey and we will watch for the female warriors. There is no harm in just watching." I remarked, turning from them and walking forward.

We passed by a line of trees and into an enormous open field. It was a gorgeous sight after trudging through the swamps and the sun was starting to come out. The air had a lovely, sweet smell to it here. The scent of flowers wafted through my nostrils, causing me to reminisce about tasting cool wine on a hot day. The air was fresh and you could hear the birds singing and crows cawing. As we walked, I tried to listen and look for the clans of fighters, but I heard nothing.

We had walked for hours through the field and a patch of woods into a flat, grassy plain. Everything turned green and the sun was still out and bright. I saw a small, crystal blue river flowing across the landscape. I looked at how the sun shimmered on the water's surface and made it look like a river of magic. I knelt on the shore and began to drink slowly with my hand. Leo did the same, as well as Franchesca. When Raphael began to drink, he splashed water everywhere and it landed all over us.

"Hey! Raphael! What in the name of the Gods!" I exclaimed, wiping the water off me. Franchesca was laughing and Leo began to chuckle as well. I finally knew what Tobit felt like. I got up and tried hard not to smile at the adorable situation. I folded my arms and stood upward. I closed my eyes and listened to the wind, though all I could hear was the sound of my friends splashing in the water and laughing like children. I turned to them and shook my head.

"Come on you fools, let's start moving again." I exclaimed, wading through the shallow river. Raphael had a nervous expression on his face, but he hesitantly tiptoed through the water. The appearance of each enormous clawed foot gracefully tapping the water made the dragon appear beyond silly for words to describe.

"Raphael, why are you tiptoeing through the water? It won't hurt you," Leo remarked with a slight giggle. Franchesca laughed along with him, shaking her head.

"Don't laugh at me! I *am* a fire dragon and I never liked water," he replied.

"We are all such a bunch of misfits," Franchesca said as she laughed, running ahead. "I can only *imagine* how we look, a fearsome dragon tiptoeing through the water, a powerful wizard who doesn't like to get his hands dirty, a wimpy knight who's scared of his own shadow, and an old witch's raven crowing above our heads."

"Ah, and you forgot one other thing Franchesca, a sarcastic cursed woman who forgets she is an overgrown black cat... who can talk!" I retorted and chuckled to myself. "Now enough, you bloody nincompoops! I will admit we are quite the motley crew, but that is what makes us so *fabulous*; wouldn't you say so, Leo?"

Leo mumbled something under his breath. "Speak for yourself, what's all this talk of a wimpy knight afraid of his own shadow?" He grumbled. "Hmph, I am not wimpy!" He complained.

"Correction then, whiney..." Franchesca pointed out as she smiled and ran further ahead of us, teasing Leo and making him flush with anger.

"Hey!" Leo shouted, "You better run! I'll skin ya for that one, Franchesca!" he shook his sword in the air as we heard her laughter echo ahead of us.

"Enough of this childish bickering! As silly as this all may look," Raphael cleared his throat trying to ignore his own desire to giggle from embarrassment. "We must remind ourselves why we are here." He scorned, continuously looking silly as he tiptoed through the water.

"Ha! Oh how I love this!" I burst out into laughter, unable to hold back and had to run through the water as Franchesca did just to get away from my crew's silly choice of words upon one another.

"Great, there he goes again! Now he'll be in a laughing fit for the next few hours! I blame YOU, Franchesca!" Leo shouted out again at her as she stood waiting for us all to make it on the other side. She pretended not to hear him and laughed as I finally made it on shore also waiting patiently for my knight and dragon to make it across. I believed Leo walked slower just to not let the dragon feel alone in his actions. *How sweet of him.*

As we continued to walk, I heard the rumble of passing horses. Gordock was above my head and began to call out to us. Did he see something? Was he warning us? When I reached the opposite shore, I continued to walk, but at a slower pace than before.

"I do not want to run into women warriors at this moment. We have to get to that tower and then to the next point on the map," I directed. My ring began to glow as I walked. In the distance, I spied a herd of horses with muscular women riding on top of them. They were screaming and yelling, making animal sounds and the Gods only knew what else.

I was frozen to the spot, looking about desperately for a place to hide. There was nothing around for miles. All I could think of was getting up on the dragon's back.

"Come on! Get on so we can get out of here!" I demanded my crew.

"Wait! What are you doing? Kain, I am not ready to fly just yet! I might not get high enough to escape!" Raphael shouted in a panic, flapping his wings.

"Raphael, listen to me, this is going to hurt, but you must try to fly for us or we lose hope in escaping at all. There are just too many of them!" I yelled back.

"Fine, I'll do what I can. Let's hope this works." Raphael cried in pain as he struggled to stretch out his hurt wings.

Leo and Franchesca swiftly climbed onto his back, assisted by his tail. He flapped his injured wings and struggled to carry us into the sky. We slowly lifted off the ground as the warriors galloped closer. The woman that appeared to be the leader pulled out a large white bow that shot an arrow directly at Raphael's heart. Raphael gave out a frightening cry.

"NO, RAPHAEL!" I cried out, holding onto him tightly as we dropped to the ground. This was horrible. The women cheered as poor Raphael fell and, deeply wounded, crashed to the ground and caused us to tumble. The world grew out of focus as I lost consciousness.

I awoke tied to a bed in a warm tent made of furs and surrounded by amber candles. My shirt was torn off and my hair lay softly over my shoulders. This did not look good. I tried to wriggle loose when a dark-haired woman walked up to me. She was holding a sharp and beautifully decorated knife. It was gold and glittered with rubies and diamonds.

"I see you have awakened, Prince Kain." Her voice was deep and sensual. She was wearing practically nothing. A leather pelt was thrown around her hips that rested high above her laced leather boots. Her chest was scantily covered by brown leather strips topped by fur around her shoulders. Her shins and forearms were protected by hardened leather armor that was lined in thin tree branches and colorful feathers. The same plumage adorned her head as a headdress. Matching war paint accentuated her chiseled features as her lips curled into a sinister smile.

"Where are my friends, you witch? I am not amused at your little game here, so let me go. I have things to do," I ordered while struggling to get loose.

She chuckled and grinned, leaning close to me and holding the knife up to my chin. Her hair was like Leo's, dark like a raven's but smooth as silk. Her skin was slightly tanned with high cheekbones and beautiful light green eyes. Her body was muscular, yet curvy. She was a delicious woman, but frightening with a weapon in her hands.

"You are a cheeky one, princy. When I am done with you, I will kill you quickly." She sprang on top of me and squeezed me between her thighs. I cannot say this didn't feel good, but I could not stop thinking about Leo and my friends.

"You have to let me go. I do not have time for any of this, woman. I will only say this once. Let me go, or I will force you," I exclaimed, now grinning to her with my most charming of smiles.

"Time? We women do not believe in it, for there is plenty to go around. You will bring me a strong daughter. Now lay still and enjoy your last moments of ecstasy like a good boy," she cooed. She began undoing my breeches. I was enchanted and slightly aroused by her strength as I watched her.

Who were these women? I could feel the heat coming from her body; she grew more excited with each squeeze of her thigh. I was weak and as much as I concentrated, I couldn't use my powers to break away. She wore a necklace that glowed brighter and brighter with every moment of her body on top of me. When I looked at it, it made me weaker. That was what was keeping me in a paralyzed state. This was not good at all. Was I really going to die here? Like this? My heart ached for Leo, though this woman was beautiful, she was going to kill me after and that was not going to work well with me in my quest. I just could not allow this woman to go any further.

My anger grew and my body felt many things all at once. Pleasure, desire, hate, and power surged through me. I closed my eyes and struggled to only think of Leo and my friends. My brother and my master's image echoed through my mind. I could feel myself growing stronger again. I opened my eyes and at that moment, right before I was going to rip the ropes that held me down, a tall, strong beautiful blond haired woman came in. She could have been my sister; her features were akin to mine and Abel's. She was the leader who shot down Raphael with the large white bow. She had polished silver armor on her shoulders, breasts, arms and legs. She wore leathers of all different colors and feathers, dangling from within her curly blond locks.

"Anita, stop this at once and bring him to my tent." The leader spoke in a deeper voice than the woman's on top of me.

"But my queen, I-" She was then cut off by her leader.

"Do as I command! Another word and you will be punished." The leader spoke more threateningly this time. She then left the tent, causing the light from the outside to disappear. Anita gazed at me sadly. She untied me and gave me back my shirt.

"Here, put that on and follow me. My queen wishes to see you within her tent. Do not try to make any moves." She continued to play with her knife and give me sad but cruel looks. "You are beautiful for a man. All the ladies from where you live must adore you. Why are out here? You should be back at your castle sipping tea."

"How do you know who I am?" I asked while lacing up my shirt.

"Everyone knows who you are," she replied. "Even out here, we have heard of the stories about you and your brother. Tales travel fast. Your brother may look like you, but you have a darker aura. It is obvious." Her head quickly turned to the entranceway. "Come, let me take you now to my queen's tent." She took me by the arm and led me outside. The sun was out and it was a bright warm day. I wondered how long I was trapped in that tent, for it looked like another day than when it was that we were caught.

There were woman everywhere dressed in furs and leathers and wearing jewelry of all kinds. Tents scattered over a grassy land and a small river flowed off in the east. I was dragged into the largest tent. The tall woman leader sat in a carved wooden chair. Her leg crossed over the other like a gentleman would sit contemplating politics, stroking her chin. She was indeed quite charming looking and was almost masculine. Her facial features were strong and sharp. Her eyes were the same color as mine. Her armor glistened with the small bits of light that peeked through the tent's holes. She was adorned in pelts, silver armor, and a long cloak made of a white furs. She was slightly taller than me, even though I was six feet tall.

Off to the right of the tent, I heard a large cat purring. When I looked into the dark shady part of the room, there I saw two large green glowing eyes. I stepped closer and noticed it was Franchesca! Her long feline body stretched out over soft pillows on the ground. She licked her paws.

"Franchesca! You're safe!" I yelled going up to her.

"Of course, my prince. I am glad you are safe as well." She nudged her head into my chest as I petted her soft fur. Her massive form lay still in my arms.

"Where are Leo and the others?" I quickly asked Franchesca as I lifted her head up to look me in the eyes.

"Leo is safe and resting. My friends are healing Raphael's wounds. He will be alright," she replied.

"Your friends? These women are your friends?" I asked with a hint of confusion but mostly in shock. I was pleased to hear this, but at the same time, anger boiled up from within me.

"I knew these women... it's a long story that I will share with you later. Morilda is allowing us to stay for the night and rest up before heading out on our journey." Franchesca purred and started to lick her paws again.

"That is fine as long as us men are not taken advantage of!" I said with annoyance, looking at the leader now known as Morilda.

"You will be safe. My girls will not harm you in any way. You have my word. If any of them do try anything, they will be punished." She spoke in a deep relaxing voice as she poured wine into two goblets. "Thirsty, young prince?"

"Yes, please," I nodded and took the goblet from her. I was parched and ravenously hungry. "May I see Leo or Raphael?" I asked, gulping my wine.

"Of course you may see Leo, but Raphael will need his rest. Franchesca can take you to him." Morilda placed her cup down on a round wooden table and sat down upon her throne. She walked over to me and placed her muscular arm over my shoulder, smirked and whispered in my ear with her deep, powerful voice. "Though, before you go, I will let you in on a little secret. You are the first man I have been attracted to in many years. I mostly fancy women and I must say, I have one on my mind right now." She smiled and looked at Franchesca and then back at me as she laughed softly. A slight feminine side to her came out as her head turned, her golden locks sliding off her shoulders and she gazed at me with her beautiful blue eyes. She was stunning like a goddess and glowing as bright as a star. Out of all the women here, I would have to say, she was the most beautiful, radiant, strongest and tallest of them all. Even I was taken aback by her unique beauty. If I was not so in love with Leo, she would be one I would give myself to. I adored her the more I stood in her presence. She was truly fabulous.

Morilda winked at me and laughed as she slid her arm off my shoulder and walked back to grab her goblet of wine from the table, took a gulp of it, then waved her hand to Franchesca. "You may show him to his handsome friend." She chuckled as her cheeks flushed from the wine and her eyes grew more dreamy and hazy.

Franchesca got up and led me down to where Leo's tent was. I thanked her as she walked back to Morilda. I wonder what was up with them two! My curiosity was getting to me but, I couldn't understand and the long story that Franchesca mentioned earlier, I wanted to know about. For now, Leo was on my mind far more. When I entered the tent, no woman was there by his side. He slept softly in a plush bed. The tent was warm. A scarlet candle burned softly in the distance. He was at peace in his dreams, for his face was relaxed and eyes were closed.

I sat next to him, but he didn't move. How handsome he was. I touched his hair and moved it softly off his sharp cheek bones. His shirt was off. I wondered if the rest of him was clothed. Scandalous thoughts and desires ran through me like crazy. Oh, how *evil* of me. A small giggle came across me as I lifted up the blankets to see if he was nude and to my surprise, he was! Oh, what a glorious sweet moment this was; I could see his sizable manhood. At that moment, Leo jumped up and grabbed both my arms. His strength was shocking. His eyes were wide as he stared at me. I gazed at him in shock, my cheeks steadily flushing red. My mouth was slightly open. My lips were glistening and our faces were only an inch away. I looked at his beautiful green eyes and wanted to move forward to place my lips gently upon his.

"Kain... my prince... by the gods, it is you. I…I am deeply sorry," he exclaimed. He let me go gently and I grinned at him.

"Oh no worries, my sweet Leo." I touched his face gently and could feel him shudder. How cute. I let my nail tease his cheek and slide down to his lips.

"Why, my prince... what are you doing?" he whispered and took my hand from his face and kissed it softly. I melted with desire. I wanted him and wanted him now. I could not wait any longer. He looked deliciously appealing on this bed. His hair was messy and wild. "Kain? Are you alright? And how is everyone else?" he asked as he looked at me with concern.

"Everyone is fine. Franchesca knows these women.

"The leader is allowing us to stay here for the night to rest up. Raphael is healing as well, but he needs his rest." I spoke softly.

"Oh... I see." He looked down and noticed he was wearing nothing. "Oh my! My clothes!" he exclaimed and looked at me with surprise.

"Don't look at me," I giggled. "I didn't take them." I held my mouth with my right hand and couldn't stop chuckling to myself.

"Great... hey, you were looking under the covers when I woke up, weren't you?" he said slyly.

"Me? Oh come now Leo, why would I do that?" I said, smiling in a sly way to him. I backed up a bit on the bed and he moved his body to follow forward towards me. He looked at me up and down and started to smile.

"I could give you many reasons, Kain." He said, then suddenly grabbed me, lifted me up, and pushed me down on my back. He lay on top of me, his body, strong and warm, kept me locked beneath him. Oh how

I wanted him to take me right now. I didn't want this moment to end.

"Could you?" I whispered back to him. He slid his arms under my back, pulling me closer to his chest. Our lips barely touched and I could feel his hot breath. My heart was skipping with delight.

"Yes..." He said, as he softly pressed his lips against mine. His tongue glided against my lips and slid into my mouth just enough to tease me. His kiss was passionate and warm. I wanted this to last. He slid his fingers through my hair and along my neck. His touch gave me goose bumps and my body fell limp into his arms. I could barely take any more.

I lifted my lips to his ear and whispered "Take me... I want you, Leo... my brave strong knight... I want you now." I heard him moan loudly and felt him turn me over with his strong arms. He was much stronger than I was; I could not fight him, but my body was weak to his touch, so even if I tried, I would fail to gain back my dominance. I could not help but submit to his moans alone, bad enough his powerful strength. From behind me he unbuckled my pants, slid them off, and placed his body on top of me as I lay naked on the bed. I was on my stomach as he kissed my shoulders and my back. He drove me crazy as he slid his manhood within me, causing me to cry out with the power of the sensation. Slowly and passionately, he took me from behind. Hours passed as he gave me sweet pleasure. I was intoxicated by his love for me. I fell asleep in his arms. He held me for hours. I drifted in and out of dreams as we lay locked together in affection. I heard him whisper before falling into a deeper sleep, "I love you Kain... I always will..."

I woke up in the middle of the night and saw Leo was out cold with his arm wrapped over my chest as he spooned me from behind. I lifted his heavy muscular arm and crawled out of the bed silently. Putting on my pants and unlaced shirt, I walked out to breathe barefoot, feeling the cold earth against my pale toes. I needed to get some fresh air. As I looked up at the stars taking in the night air, I heard a sound coming from the leader's tent nearby. Within the light of the tent, you could see a silhouette of a big cat and image of a woman. I tiptoed over to the tent where a small hole shined bright candlelight through it. I could not help myself but to peek into the hole.

I wonder what Franchesca is doing at the leader's tent at such an hour. How can they know each other and why did Morilda smile at Franchesca when mentioning a woman she had her eyes on?

As I pushed my eye up against the rip in the fabric of the tent, I heard more closely a woman moaning and there was her beautiful strong thighs, the thighs of Morilda and her legs up high as she lay beautifully upon silk and velvet, gold and wine colored pillows. My eyes widened when I caught the image of Franchesca between Morilda's warm thighs, her eyes looking at the warrior Queen seductively as she stroked her large catlike tongue up and down the leader's sparkling wet female sex.

Oh my, *this* was something I wasn't expecting! They shared affection as Leo and I do? I had no idea! I continued to watch perversely as Morilda's body fell into the submission of the pleasure Franchesca gave her. Such a strong female arching her back, her head, with golden locks draping behind her and with her strong arms, she held the head of her beautiful feline friend as both rocked to one another's rhythms. Morilda's body withered and became weak, submitting all her strength, her pride and power over to Franchesca as she moved her body back and forth, riding the cat's tongue and delicious motions. I was getting slightly aroused watching such things but felt it was wrong for me to interfere or watch their intimate moment, as strange as it was, I was nowhere near to judge. Perhaps Franchesca knew Morilda when she was once human? Perhaps it was then they caught affections for one another? I wonder if Franchesca will ever tell me of this moment or of her feelings for this beautiful queen of such powerful women?

I watched the last bits of pleasure escape Morilda's lips as she moaned and collapsed her beautiful body upon the soft pillows. Franchesca walked over to lay beside her and I glowed with smiles as I turned to walk away blushing from the performance I was so lucky, yet rudely to catch out of my own foolish curiosity. *Ah Kain, when will you ever learn?* I giggled to myself as I entered back into the tent and crawled into bed with Leo. His warm body felt good against my cold skin. *I shall dream interesting things tonight!* I thought as I closed my eyes and fell softly to sleep in the arms of my handsome knight.

When I awoke in the morning, I could hear the birds singing and a dragon roaring outside of our tent. Leo and I must have slept in during the commotion. I got dressed and stepped outside, just to notice Raphael being cared for and washed by a band of half-naked women, laughing and holding buckets of water as they tossed it on him. I laughed, looking up at him as I clapped my hands and shouted. "Early bath, my friend?" I laughed harder as he snarled at me.

"Funny! You know how much I hate this Kain, call them off! I hate water." He shouted as he puffed out some smoke from his nose.

"Ah, I would if I could, but I am not the one in charge here, looks like you are on your own." I chuckled as I threw some water from a bucket on my face to help myself wake up. Drying my face with my shirt, I noticed Leo stepped out of the tent. *Ah, look at him, he's so cute in the morning with his hair all messy, small bit of stubble on his chin and eyes all groggy*. The body of a man but heart of a young boy, I glowed as I smiled at him. Taking some water from a bucket in my hand, I splashed it at him while he yawned, shocking him as he showed signs of annoyance.

"Kain! What did you do that for??" He shouted as he rubbed the water off his face. I laughed and blushed already loving this day even further.

"Oh hush, Leo! You were being a big sleepyhead, I just could not help myself. It's only water, stop whining!" I giggled to myself as I stormed off to look for Franchesca. I could not help but wonder how her interesting night went with the queen of the warriors. Oh how this was turning out to be such a wonderful day. The dragon was being cleaned and washed, making his crystal body shine and gleam in the yellow sunlight. The warrior women were even more gorgeous as they bounced and giggled, covered in soapy water, I could not help but blush red watching their delicious bodies clean the grumpy dragon. Leo and I had one of the best nights ever since we met. Franchesca I am sure has many secrets to share and I, being one nosy perverted fool, just *had* to know more of her and the warrior Queen.

What a day! The air from the forest was crisp and I could smell roasted meat and cooked eggs coming from a giant wooden lodge. A rosy, plump, curvy but lovely lady came out of the lodge doors and shouted to the other girls.

"Breakfast is ready ladies, come and get it!!" Thc woman shouted as the entire fleet of women flocked towards the lodge, dropping their buckets and cheering happily. *A man could get to really enjoy this place.* I thought as I shook my head smiling and followed the women into the lodge to see what was cooking. My stomach growled as the smell of the roasted meat grew stronger. Fresh breads, cheeses and cooked eggs lay across a large long table as the women crowded around slamming their forks and knives down hard cheering for the meat to be served. I was laughing at how jolly and masculine these women were but yet they were so beautiful. Such barbarism and wild customs they had. The leader, Morilda, sat at the end of the table on a plush, fancy carved wooden chair painted in gold and magnificent colors. She gave me such wonderful flashbacks to how she was last night, but here she sat like a king on a throne. One arm rested upon the arm of the chair, her fist slightly close to her chin, legs widely spread as she leaned back comfortably and the other arm rested upon the table. She smirked and grinned at the shouts and happy calls for meat from her warriors. She then raised her hand in the air and the room went silent.

There I stood, watching her and the crew. Morilda stood from her chair and raised her glass in the air. "Please, everyone, let us welcome our guests to feast and dine with us this beautiful morning." She waved for me and surprisingly Leo who stood behind me, to come forward and take a seat at the feasting table. Two chairs awaited our presence and so we filled them while smiling to the ladies who smiled back. I noticed then that Franchesca was laying on the ground by the Queen's chair resting her head upon her feet. I blushed and bowed my head just to have it rise again as women cheered and rose their glasses. Enormous plates of roasted meats came out with servant girls holding them and placing them upon the table. The women continued to cheer and without hesitation, grabbed roasted legs and pork from the table with their bare hands.

"Let the feast begin!" Morilda shouted as she smiled down to Franchesca and fed her by hand a large piece of meat, then patted her head gently, just to glide her large hand down to stroke Franchesca's furry cheek and soon under her chin, ever so gracefully. Franchesca purred loudly, seductively looking up at her warrior Queen. *Such affection shined with those two. Something special that made even my heart skip. I adored Morilda and Franchesca, both, those women were stealing my heart in a loving way. I myself could not help but fall in love with them both, but it will be Leo who always holds that. The second I see him I melt, I have to keep myself under control around him and try hard not to show signs of my desire for him so often now. Even if we did have our moments last night, I am still the one in charge here and his prince. I can't have him thinking he has any control over me now.* I giggled to myself as a piece of meat waved fiercely in front of my face. I was about to burst out laughing until I found the leg of meat shoved into my mouth and I looked at the woman who did it with stunned eyes. Leo burst out into tears of laughter.

"Haha! That ought to shut him up!" Leo held his stomach and chuckled hard, slamming the table with his fist.

I looked at him angrily. Pulling it from my mouth and smacked him across the face with the meat, then smirked and took a bite.

"Yes and it's great to teach others respect." I smirked and took a big bite of the flesh from the juicy bone. He glared at me and rubbed his jaw. *Poor thing, I must really annoy him, but I find it so fun, it's probably the evil within me. Heheh.*

We finished our meal and I was incredibly full. I had trouble getting up from the table which felt like a whole day of sitting, talking, eating and drinking. I was flushed with joy as Leo helped me get up and out of the lodge, holding onto my elbow and being the gentleman he was, guiding me out. When I stepped outside, Raphael was healed, cleaned and awaiting for us to continue onwards towards our destination. Gordock flew over to my shoulder and screeched in my ear, causing me to jump a bit nervously. Leo, holding back his chuckles, turned away. Franchesca was still with the leader as she looked up at her. You could see how much she didn't want to leave her side and I could say the same for Morilda. After many minutes, Franchesca walked over to me and spoke calmly.

"You still hold your promise to me, Kain? That you will help me return to my human form?" She said sadly as she looked low to the ground. A small tear released itself from her beautiful eye and glided gently down her fuzzy soft cheek. I knelt down on one knee, wiping the wet tears from her eye and cheek.

"Of course I hold that promise and I will return you back to your human form. You have my word, my dear." I said as I smiled to her and she licked my hand gently.

"Thank you Kain, you are a greater prince than many may believe. You are truly worthy of the destiny that awaits you." She whispered and closed her eyes rubbing her head against my same hand she licked. Such a beauty she was. I truly meant my words to her and she had trusted me, gone so far with me through this journey that I could never forgive myself if I didn't keep to my word. I want to see her human again and I felt I was not the only one.

Looking at Franchesca from afar was Morilda and for the first time I saw her showing a sad emotion. Her eyes were glassy as she held back her affections or even the desire to run over and never let Franchesca go. She ignored that part of her, stood off in the distance and held herself up strong. Franchesca could not even look back, her eyes filled up with more tears and she did not question why I didn't ask about her feelings. She did not care to ask for it was as if she knew that I knew what was wrong, and I did.

Don't you worry your beautiful head my gentle kitten, I will make sure your curse is removed and that you may see your warrior woman again. That I also promise.

Chapter Eleven
The Crystal Tower

The night sky was glowing like crystals in a cave as it twinkled above us. The sky was a rich dark black and blue and the air was cool. We were high up on Raphael as he flew us quickly across the lands below. We had all moved out of the vision of the warrior women hours ago. I looked at my ring, which began to glow more powerfully than before. "We must be very close to the Tower," I said softly.

"We should land because Roland said that we cannot see the Tower from above the ground." Franchesca suggested, licking her paw slowly. Raphael then flew down to a woodland grove that was littered with blue fireflies, exactly as I had seen in my vision. We landed softly and jumped off of the dragon's back. As I explored the area, I noticed that this was no ordinary forest. I looked at the trees and saw they were not made of leaves and wood. Instead, the plant and animal life glistened like glass.

"What is going on here? What have we walked into?" I asked, turning to face everyone.

"More like fly into, my prince." Leo remarked, laughing to himself.

"Oh aren't you the joker," I replied, shaking my head as Leo continued to snicker.

"Not all jokes are for you, Kain." He said, walking over to one of the trees. I rolled my eyes and continued to stare at the ground. I spotted a path ahead, illuminated by the ring. I turned my face up and shivered; it was cold here.

"Let's follow this pathway." I said softly. I looked at my ring and it glowed steadily brighter as we walked and after only minutes, we came across an eerie mist. A tense vibration resonated from it, as if it served as a doorway to a world unknown.

"What the hell is that?" Leo said, touching the fog and watching his hand disappear.

"The other side must be the Crystal Forest. I heard everything is made of crystal there, even the animals." Raphael said.

"Wait, you knew something about this and you didn't tell us?" I shouted and looked back at Raphael.

"I must have forgotten up until now! Seeing it just now jogged my memory! Sorry about that." He laughed to himself. I shook my head and rolled my eyes.

"Some help you are, dragon!" I said turning to face the strange mist.

"Hey! I flew you here and now we await your command." He replied with a louder voice puffing out smoke from his nostrils.

"Quiet you two, this is no time for bickering. We should really stay focused, plus, I don't like the feeling of this place," Whispered Franchesca as she lowered her head and body in a panic looking around nervously.

"Now look who's afraid of their own shadow? Don't be such a *scardy-cat*, Miss Ktty. Puuuuuuur," Leo said sarcastically, reminding Franchesca of her snarky comment from the other day.

"Ha ha, very funny," she growled back with the same amount of sarcasm as Leo.

"Enough! No one is to give orders or be an *ass* here other than *me*! Now, what are we waiting for? Let's walk through this thing already!" I exclaimed, watching Leo blush and walking through it slowly. I closed my eyes and when I felt myself reach the other side, I opened my eyes to witness white snowflakes falling in front of me. I held out my hands to feel them melt upon my skin; it was beautiful. Leo followed behind me as he appeared from the mist and he gazed in wonder at the breathtaking sight. The forest was covered in snow. As I approached the trees, my eyes were entranced by the way each one shone, like transparent pearls in the moonlight. I touched a nearby trunk and felt its impeccable smoothness; I knew then that the plant life here was indeed made of crystal. There were birds flying around and they were made of crystal as well. I could not believe how spectacular it was.

"Look at this place, Leo. Have you ever seen anything so beautiful?" I asked him.

He shook his head and whispered, "I could name something or should I say someone." He chuckled to himself and looked at the ground to push the snow away. The earth was crystal as well as the rocks. Franchesca and Raphael stood behind Leo. I began to follow the pathway and up ahead could see the large crystal Tower forming in the distance.

"Look! There it is!" I yelled, starting to run up to it. Leo followed behind me along with Franchesca and Raphael. As I sprinted along the crystal path, I wondered what the tower held. As I approached, I saw the tower shine with iridescent color in the moonlight; wherever light hit, a beam reflected in a rainbow range of hues. There were two statues of horses on either side of the entrance with glassy horns, causing them to resemble unicorns. Whoever carved these beautiful sculptures was highly skilled for they looked extremely real. I came upon a towering set of double doors that glistened magnificently. I placed my hand on the ornate crystal door handle, but was halted by a lurch from behind me. At that moment, I spied out of the corner of my eye the unicorns began to move! Their eyes glowed with an icy blue color. I stepped back and they devilishly walked towards me. They did not look happy or welcoming.

"What did you do now, Kain?" Leo whispered in a panicked voice.

I whispered back at him, "I have no clue. All I did was put my hand on the handle of the door." He then pulled out his sword and I did the same as the unicorns trotted toward us. "Great, what do we do now? These creatures look unstoppable." I said, standing steadfast and staring at them both. I thought that I could try talking to them telepathically.

"Maybe if I tell them we mean no harm, they will let us pass?" I whispered smiling nervously to Leo as we held our swords pointed directly at them and Franchesca by our side, hissing.

"Oh yes! Great idea, as if they will let us go in for being polite with words. I'm sorry my prince, but I don't believe this is a place where your charm will work." Leo whispered back fiercely.

"Well, we got nothing to lose. I might as well give it a shot!" I said as I grinned at him. Shutting my eyes, I concentrated, willing my telepathic words to pass onto the statues. All of a sudden, they halted in their tracks and stared at us. Leo and I both loosened up our grips on our sword hilts and looked at each other curiously. The unicorns turned and walked calmly back to the tower.

"What did you say to them?" Leo stammered.

"Why, I actually said nothing at all!" I replied quickly and confused.

"What? Then why did they leave us be?" He whispered.

"I honestly have no idea!" I spoke back and when I was about to speak again, I noticed a haunting voice call my name as the doors opened to the crystal tower entrance.

All of us looked at one another. “Raphael, you stay out here and stand guard, we will go in. The sword must be here!” I mentioned as I walked up to the front door and entered the tower.

“Kaaaaiiinnn...” The voice spoke again as it echoed the beautiful crystal walls. “Only Kain may enter, the rest of you must wait outside!” The voice continued to hiss hauntingly.

I turned to my friends and Leo with confusion and concern upon my face but I knew that I must do as the voice commanded or he could hurt them. I nodded to Leo and Franchesca as I took Gordock off my shoulder and asked him kindly to follow them.

“Don’t worry my friends, I shall return to you, with the sword. I will not be long. Trust me.” I smiled to them as the doors to the entrance of the tower closed and I no longer saw them or heard them after. I turned then to face another door in which a transparent blue hooded figure stood before me. I jumped back pulling out my sword in defense to my shocked reaction.

“No need for your weapon here, it is useless.” The voice spoke and I watched my sword vanish into a puff of blue smoke. I wanted to say something in rage against him for removing my sword from my hands but I stayed quiet. I watched him closely until he too vanished before my eyes. The doors opened behind him as white marble stairs were revealed behind it, curling upwards into a spiral that felt miles to walk up.

I walked and walked up each step, turning more exhausted as the time went by. I do not know how many minutes passed that I had to climb those stairs, but right when I could not take it anymore, I came to a golden door, one of the tallest I had ever seen. It had such intricate details carved into it. Ancient writing, a symbol of a sword and red stoned necklace appeared before me in what seemed to be a story of two warriors who are meant to be chosen in a tale of evil and greed. I could not make out all of it, but it showed a great city, a king and queen and a boy and girl who it kept repeating were chosen to unlock the secrets of a great power hidden within their own blood.

I spoke a few cabalistic words to allow some golden fire to glow in my hand so I could capture more of the story but as I grew closer to make out the words and images, the doors opened. To my amazement, it revealed an enormous room with a ceiling that was not viewable from my level. This was no longer a tower of crystal, but a tower of white marble. A bright light shined above, illuminating a white throne, red fabric for the cushion with carvings of a man and a woman on either side, crafted into the back of the chair holding their arms up and pointing to the endless ceiling of this magnificent tower. Everything was white, gold and red in this room. The floor I walked on was a white shiny marble, reflecting the beautiful walls with carvings of people and human bodies fused into it. Each figure reached and stretched up over one another as if crawling up the wall, struggling to get to the top.

My breath was taken away as I stared at each person; each human was sculpted with their own unique features and qualities. One could think they were not sculptures at all. I suddenly gulped with fear as a terrible feeling came over me, believing for a second that they were not sculptures, but indeed real people, that were once human but attempted to climb to the top only to become part of the wall. I walked up to the throne, but I dared not sit upon it. I knew better not to take that chance for everything here did not seem right. I looked up again which made me want to fall backwards. The circular room with curved walls that reached high up disappeared into a point which made the ceiling not visible. When I stared into the light coming from the top, it only made me curious, so curious that I wanted only to climb to the top and find out where that beautiful light was coming from. It was like looking into the light of the Gods. I could not resist the urge to see what was up the tower. No stairs were available, no ladder or ropes. The warm light beat down upon my face like a light I never felt before. It embraced my body and filled my mind with soothing feelings. The magic in my body felt as if it were being filled up and restored. I felt healed, awakened by the light and my curiosity was growing. I wanted to get closer, to see more of this light and I only ached more to be engulfed within it. I lost track of time, and even the thought and memory of my friends waiting for me outside.

It was as if I was being possessed by the light and the urge to climb the wall became stronger to me. I couldn't fight it any longer as I walked up to a section of the wall that had a woman reaching upwards from it. The rest of her body fused within it as her arms reached upwards and her soft white breasts gently rested from her chest. I walked up closer to her until suddenly her body began to move. I stepped backwards in fear, shouting and when I cried, my voice echoed off the walls, awakening the sculptures that reached high along the tower.

The room filled with moving fused marble beings along the perimeter, circling high up into the unseen ceiling. When I looked up, a haunting image of the bodies waved like an ocean rippling. The arms, the legs and any limbs of the people made the illusion that the tower was alive. My heart began to beat fast but my urge to climb was still overcoming my body. *I needed to fight it!* I closed my eyes and stepped out of the light.

When I opened my eyes again, I saw that same woman, reaching out to me now, her arms stretching and fingers reaching for dear life as she opened her mouth, releasing no sound. A frightening image to witness which gave me chills down my spine. *Gods, get me out of here*! I shouted in my thoughts. *What horrid place is this?*

The urge to climb still drove me but I covered my ears, fell to my knees on the cold marble floor and shut my eyes. I began to shout loudly trying to fight the possession and take back control of my body. I shouted so loudly that the walls began to shake, the people that moved, stuck into the wall started to crack. I looked at them for a second peeking just a bit as they cracked further and turned to glittering dust. Every being shattered along the wall like glass, just to turn to a shimmering dust where even the dust vanished into nothing and silence followed.

No more walls shook, my voice no longer echoed and everything was deathly quiet. Loneliness came over me, so great that it made me feel sick. I held my stomach in fear and began to shake. *What is happening to me?* I thought as I drew images of my friends and Leo. I had forgotten how long it had been. I could not even remember why I was here anymore until a ghostly figure appeared before me. It was the same one from before. His image reminded me of a lost memory. I had started to lose myself in this place.

"I see you avoided the temptation to climb. Impressive, you are the first of many to ever succeed." The voice calmly whispered. As he spoke, it was as if my life was returning to me, my very soul. "You are different Kain, you are worthy of the sword, but you must know that the only thing you should fear... is yourself." He tilted his head creepily from side to side before speaking slowly again, looking down at me. "But it is you who must show me now just what you truly stand for!" He said in a harsher tone as his blue robed body turned and lifted his arm forward. His fingers revealed a woman of pale skin. There she stood by the entrance, smiling at me.

"Your mother wishes to speak to you..." The hooded figure answered.

"My mother? I... but she is dead!" I replied to him with tears in my eyes. "What kind of sick joke are you playing here? Stop it! Stop showing me her! She is dead! DEAD!" I raised my fist at him and his voice stopped me.

"Calm yourself Kain, this place is connected to the realm of the dead; she wishes to speak to you." He replied again and pointed directly at her once again. I could not believe him but if he was telling the truth, this would give me my time to speak to her. I turned towards her direction and faced her. What a beautiful woman she was, so radiant and glowing. I did not feel worthy to be in her presence. *What a terrible son I have been, how could I have let Arius kill her and never know about it! How could I have been such a fool? My heart felt torn, what a monster I am. What a monster I have become.*

"Shhhh... Do not say such things, my son." She spoke with such a soothing tone. It softly echoed in the room and the light her body gave off was the same light that came from the top of the tower.

I walked closer to her as she held open her arms to me. Tears leaked from my eyes uncontrollably. I was beginning to lose myself again but this time, all I wanted was to be in her arms and nothing could stop me, not even myself.

"Mother... I'm sorry, I'm so sorry." Was all that I could say as I placed my head on her chest and hugged her tight. It felt a lifetime I held her in my arms. She stroked my hair and whispered in my ear gently.

"It is alright... just know that I love you no matter what. Keep that heart, hold my love for you there and you will always be strong. Do not lose yourself Kain, you and Abel both hold a gift far greater than power in this world. The gift... of love. With it, you will always be strong, always be great. It is what binds us humans to all that is living. It is what a human searches for most and sometimes without realizing it. It is what keeps us going, what drives us, what keeps us alive. Hold onto it for as long as you live, for it will always be with you after, even in death. It is the greatest gift anyone could ever ask for and I gave it to you and your brother. I love you Kain... I always will." And as she said those words, I remembered Leo said the same words to me. My eyes hurt from the amount of salty tears that dripped down my cheeks. She looked into my eyes and kissed my forehead. I was speechless and gazed into her eyes further when I saw her beautiful radiant face grow sad and in pain as I witnessed her grow weak in my arms. She looked over and pointed at a tall dark figure as she shouted out in horror.

"Mother! MOTHER! What is wrong? Please..." I cried as I tried to help her up but there stood in the shadows, my master, Arius, laughing.

"YOU BASTARD! I HATE YOU!! LEAVE HER ALONE!" I shouted as I charged at him with my hands in tight fists. My teeth were bared, my eyes shadowed by my dark eyebrows that came together in a fierce look. I lost control of myself. Hate, anger and rage soared through my veins like poison yet fuel. I went berserk, where all my thoughts were lost in images of me tearing him apart, limb by limb.

I jumped high in the air towards him and landed with my fists hard at his face when suddenly he vanished into a puff of blue smoke. My eyes were bugging out of my skull, where I had to control myself just to stand up. My rage had my body were shaking, my muscles tense and bulging. My hands formed into a claw formation which reflected a red glare from my eyes. I looked at the floor and there I saw my reflection just to cause a quick reaction to cover my eyes with my hands. I tried to calm myself and look up to see if my mother was alright, but she was gone. Nothing but darkness surrounded me with an image now that stood with light beaming down upon it. The image of a tall, dark man with long hair looked at me with glowing red eyes. I looked closer as he stepped further into the light.

"You have changed, Kain. You are a fool to turn down Ariaus's wishes. The death of your mother was worth everything so that you could learn the ways of dark magic. You would not have the power you have if it was not for Ariaus. He taught you everything he knew, treated you like a son, raised you! Took you away from a family that did not care about you and only your brother, the goodie-goodie golden haired boy was important enough to rule over *your* kingdom! He is weak, and look now, you have grown to be as weak as him. You are a fool to turn down such power. You and I could have it all! Together, we could have eternity! But no, instead, you choose to be a weak fool, letting your emotions get to you. You are not worthy of Sceptor's powers! What kind of weak fool have you become?" He spoke with the same voice as my own. Dressed in the same clothing, far neater looking than I. His hair was neatly tied back as mine was looser. His eyes were red, skin so pale he appeared dead, cold and nonexistent. His hair was raven black. *And then it became clear why, it was me*!

"You are wrong!" I shouted as I charged at him as he pushed me back with a force of power I could not defend from. My body flew across the dark room.

"Am I? Haha, who is wrong when it is your body that cannot fight this power I have? Look at you! Crawling and begging for your mommy to protect you. How pathetic! You should forget her and come back to me, become one with me! There is no pain here, no fear, no dirty feelings to care of others. It makes you weak! It is better to just care for yourself for those who claim to care for you are liars!" He spoke as his hands lit up with blue flames that he tossed towards me, surrounding me in their heat, creating a ring I could not escape from. "No one cares about you like I do, Kain! No one deserves this power for they are all weak. You were chosen to have it and you turn it down for foolish emotions! You betray Ariaus, yourself and your own power that was given to you as a gift! What fool turns down such power? I should destroy you now, let only I control your body and destroy this weaker part that should have never been born in the first place!" He shouted as he tossed a force of hot flames directly at me.

"YOU ARE THE WEAK ONE!" I shouted loudly as I built up a power of light to shield me from his flames. I then forced it back into his direction. I thought about Leo and Franchesca. How she wants to be human again, be with her female lover and end her curse. How Raphael risked his life and took his time to get us here. How Leo whispered to me that night as he held me, how he loves me and always will. The light I conjured grew larger as it flew into his body, forcing him to the ground. I jumped through the flames and landed on top of him.

"It is you who is weak! You need this power in order to feel needed in this world! You who cries at the thought of being alone yet surrounding yourself with loneliness and nothing but the power within you to keep you company! Your jealousy of your own brother blinds you! You hate him for no reason! You fear the pain that comes with love. You know nothing of it. You fear it so much that it weakens you! So weak to the fear of love, that you rather destroy it than have it torture your own selfish already broken heart.

"You would rather wish it never existed and even if that meant taking it away from others, then so be it! How weak is that to fear something like love. To fear caring for others or losing them! You are the weak one. YOU!" I shouted at his face as I held him down. He looked up at me in fear, my tears dripped all over him. All over myself. I hated him so much but it was not his fault. He was scared, scared of all the pain and feelings he was afraid to deal with. One so weak only needs one thing. I took him into my arms and laid there holding him. He fought me, but I did not care. I was willing to die to protect him. I was willing to die to stop him just if it meant Leo and the others would be left alone in peace, without something so horrible in the world to take away their goodness, their love and very being of greatness. I wanted to protect them, protect the goodness in them and in me. If it meant me dyeing, then so be it.

I held onto him tight, forgiving him, yet loving him at the same time, letting my hate and anger melt away. I knew that evil is built from pain and hurt and fear. I knew now that this monster within me could be tamed if only love were to hold him down. *My mother is right... she is more than right.* I felt myself slipping into him and we became one as I felt my belly, arms, legs and cheekbones glided gently to the floor.

I laid there in tears, watching my tears roll off my chin and hit the cold polished floor beneath me. I felt as if I had fallen asleep, but I could not tell. My eyes opened and I saw my reflection in the floor that now was stained with my tears. Blue eyes looked back at me and my image. My hair was undone and unkempt looking. I looked horrid, but there was something beautiful about it at the same time, something deep down I could not explain.

I felt happy and free. I wanted to kiss the floor with joy, kiss my reflection but I giggled to myself instead thinking of how silly it would be. *Was it all a dream?* I thought out loud as I looked around curiously. The room was no longer dark and I could see the figures were back along the wall again. I ignored them and I even ignored the urge to climb the tower for it did not torture me as it did before. My mind was focused again. All I could think about was getting out of the tower and seeing Leo's handsome face, hearing the purring of Franchesca as she licked my hand and the screeching of Gordock as he rested upon my shoulder. Even that silly dragon made me chuckle in thought of greeting him and imagining how wonderful a feeling it is to ride on his back with my friends.

I didn't want these thoughts to ever end and it made me want to shed more tears but I felt exhausted and dry. These tears were different though, ones I would shed out of joy and happiness. A feeling of pride came over me. I was proud of myself, proud of what I had done and felt awakened from a nightmare, a grasp on my soul that never should have been there. *I was wrong all these years and now, I feel I am ready to face anything and anyone.*

I got up off the floor and looked at the door from the room. I didn't want to be here anymore, just to be with my friends, for they mean everything to me. When I reached my hand for the door handle, I heard a sound behind me.

"Aren't you forgetting something Kain?" A haunting, familiar voice echoed. I turned to see who it was and of course, the blue hooded figure stood before me. He removed his hood and there... there stood an image of a handsome golden haired man. He eerily resembled the warrior queen from the female tribe. Their features seemed so uniquely similar I could have sworn they were related. "Don't you want to know where to find the sword?" He asked calmly. My mind was so focused on seeing everyone again that I had completely forgotten the entire reason to which I came here.

"I honestly... had forgotten, but I do believe I should know. I want to prevent it from falling into the wrong hands if possible. Unless you believe it will be safe here." I mentioned to him as he looked at me and smiled. He looked as if he was in his late thirties. He had lightly tanned skin, perfectly blond wavy hair and bright blue eyes just like Morilda. So stunning to look at yet, he was transparent and glowing. White ancient writing was painted all over his blue robe and I could see where some white armor hid beneath the fabric. He was stunning, like a knight he stood there, brave and staring at me with big blue eyes. I was lost in him. Something about his presence was comforting.

"Heh.. heh.. How interesting you mention such things. I am impressed with you Kain. You are worthy of the sword I once held, but as you can see, I no longer can do so." He laughed softly to himself. Such a warm smile and kind eyes he had, that he eased my nerves with every friendly gaze at me. "You must know that the sword is not here but elsewhere, within a castle not too far from this realm. The sword was once owned by me until I lost it during a great search I was on for my captured sister. It was many years ago, when my sister was captured by an evil sorceress queen. The sword belonged to my father and it held an ancient power.

"I was then cursed by the sorceress queen who condemned me into this crystal tower, never to know of my physical body ever again. Like a spirit, I wander this tower and live within this realm unable to exit. Before she did so, a great wizard who was like a father to me placed a counter spell on her curse, took my sword that was unable to come into this realm and placed a counter spell upon the sword. It was inscribed that a hero of equal power to my own will come to get the sword that I had lost, but he or she must be worthy to wield it and only then, it will set me free from this spiritual prison and my body can be once again returned to physical form. Of course there is a risk for my wizard friend could only do what he could. The bad side to this is, if I were to ever wield the sword again, I would die and soon after my soul would be returned here, trapped to wander this realm for eternity. So with that, I only ask you this, Kain, wield that sword wisely and if for any reason I come in contact with you, keep it far from myself so that may never happen. Once the sword is yours, it is yours forever and your soul is then merged with it."

"So the sword once belonged to you? Who... who are you?" I asked, squinting my eyes out of great curiosity. He smiled and looked down for second, then back up at me.

"I am Mandel, one of the chosen, destined to save our planet, Noven, from a terrible darkness. I am the last of a bloodline lost that once thrived here on our planet hundreds of years ago. I know, when I reunite with my sister, I will achieve this and put a stop to the ones who still seek our power for evil. The ones who seek it will use the power wrongly and possibly destroy us all, including the planet we live upon. You have a good heart within you, Kain. It does not matter what dark power exists within you, for it is the way you wield it that truly matters. Now go! You are running out of time." He pointed at my pocket, which held my map folded up inside. “The map should guide you now to the sword. I marked it for you. Just follow the new path in that direction and you should get there. Be careful, it is dangerous and you may cross the Desert of Fears which could have you placed within another test of your mind.”

I took it out and looked at it. A new area began to show itself on the map. A castle appeared near the edge. “We are not far. I must find this sword before it falls into the wrong hands.” I said to myself, folding it up and placing it back into my pocket. “Thank you Mandel, I will never forget your help, I hope I may see you again and do not fear, I will keep the sword far from your presence when that time comes. I will set you free of this spiritual prison and hope that you reunite with your sister. Good luck!” I said as I quickly made my way to the door, I heard his voice echo as I exited down the stairs.

“Same to you my friend... the same to you!” his voice faded as I left the crystal tower. The air was crisply upon my face which was flushed and heated from the run down the stairs and through the tower halls. I was never so happy to see everyone as much as I was at this moment. There they stood: my friends, Leo, and even the silly dragon. I had a lot to answer for, especially since I did not even know how long I been gone.

“Kain!” Leo shouted as he jumped off the ground by a fire as he charged towards me and wrapped his big strong handsome arms around my body. He kissed me. His face felt rougher than usual which I did not mind at all. He kissed me so hard, I could feel his teeth behind his lips and his tongue slip gently into my mouth. I closed my eyes, enjoying his embrace and sweet lips. There was nothing I wanted more at this minute than this.

He moved his lips back just a bit so he could speak. "I was ready to barge down those doors if you had not come out by now! It has been a week since you've been in there! I dared not try to go in. We all grew so frightened that something had happened to you! Oh Kain, I never thought I would see you again. I feared you were dead!" He said as he pressed his head close to my chest and hugged me again more forcefully. I laughed and opened my eyes wider as I felt him squeeze my body tightly.

"I was gone for a week?" I asked still confused how so much time had passed without me even noticing.

"Yes! You did not realize? Just what happened to you in there??" He asked as he looked at me confused.

"Dear gods, long story my friend, I will tell it to you on our way to getting the sword. It is not located here. We must get out of this realm and find our way towards a castle that holds the sword within it. Though, I will say, that I almost lost myself in there."

"We were plotting a way to get in, but the crystal unicorns would come to life every time we tried to get close to the doors. It was Franchesca who believed your heart still beat and that you were safe. Somehow she knew, but I was losing my patience and trying to find another way into the tower. Please promise me you will never do that to me again!" He shouted and pointed his finger at my nose. I giggled at his actions.

"Don't you worry your handsome head. I don't think I'll be doing that again anytime soon." I replied charmingly. "Can you promise me something Leo?"

"What is that Kain?" he answered warmly.

"*Do* do something about that beard." I mentioned, grinning foolishly, pushing him aside, laughing to myself.

Chapter Twelve
The Gates of Massimilla

I soaked in the beauty of this forest, but it was getting chilly and I wanted to get out of it as fast as I got in. I saw a cloud of thick fog in front of me again. "This must be the way out of this place." I said softly to my friends.

"Let's go through it then and get out of here," Franchesca replied, walking through it. I did the same and Leo followed with Raphael passing at the rear. We walked through the portal to the sight of a dull, ashen forest. The trees were dead and there was no life in sight. Bones scattered across the ground; they must have been the skeletons of dead animals and men who tried to cross here. I had to gasp for breath; the air was thick and thoroughly unpleasant. Even Gordock struggled to fly higher than shoulder level.

"What is this place?" I asked softly. I pulled out my map and looked at it. Beyond the Crystal Tower, which was marked by drawings of twin unicorns, the map revealed a desolate area with a skull and cross-bones sigil.

"Does that symbol mean we dig our graves here?" Leo asked, pointing it. I looked at him like he was stupid and grinned, revealing my teeth.

"You're a fool; we are not going to die. All we have to do is quickly get to the next point on the map. Raphael, take us upward and onward!" I exclaimed, pushing Leo out of the way and leaping onto the dragon's back, followed by each of my friends. Raphael flapped his wings powerfully, yet he could not lift more than a few feet off the ground. He struggled, still visibly in pain from strained muscles and his still healing wounds, until he weakly landed onto the ground.

"What's wrong, Raphael?" I asked with concern.

"I cannot fly here," he responded in dismay. "The air is heavy and my wings can barely lift me. I'm grievously sorry, my prince."

"It's not your fault, my friend," I replied. "We will have to walk the rest of the way until you are able to fly again."

After hopping back on the ground, I started walking along the pathway and ignored the bones that littered the soil. Everyone followed behind and I watched to see if something was up ahead. The area had a sickening smell to it. All we could hear was the wind blowing slowly and a few dead leaves rustling along the dry ground. I had an ominous feeling about this place; the air was stagnant, yet pulsating with anticipation, as if the horrors under the soil would leap out at us at any moment. This would be too easy if we were to simply walk through this unscathed.

We walked for days in this filthily eerie landscape, taking breaks and watching each other's backs while we slept. Midway into the third day of travel, I pulled out some dry meat that I had in my pouch. I was chewing on my food when I thought I heard something. I stopped and looked around. I saw nothing and I continued my way on the path.

"Can I have some of that meat, Kain?" Leo asked me softly.

"Of course you can," I replied with a delicious grin on my face, hinting toward other means and turning around to give him some. I was then hit in the back of my head. I fell to the ground, paralyzed with pain.

I awoke to the sound of Gordock cawing frantically beside me. As I struggled to open my eyes, I spotted Leo fighting human skeletons that brandished swords and shields. As my vision regained its sharpness, I realized that these skeletons were not made of bone; they were made of wood. *What the hell were these things?* I shook my head and got up as fast as I could. I pulled out my sword and swung at the one that was fighting Leo. Raphael blew fire at them, causing them to flail and roll upon the dry ground in flames as Franchesca mauled them with her claws. I was lost in the battle and still disoriented from the blow to my head. I pushed Leo out of the way and began to fight one of the strange beasts. I sliced my sword through its skeletal frame and watched him fall apart. Even defeated, its body still twitched as it hit the ground, struggling to reassemble itself.

I knew then that I had to use my power to help burn these bloody monsters; they did not die by sword alone. I used my mind to launch fireballs at them. It worked quite well as I grabbed Leo's hand and started running down the path as several skeletons burst into flames. As more of them charged at us, I continued to combust them. My magic was growing far more powerful. Waving my arms forward, I propelled our attackers backward through the air. As I ran out of the dark forest with everyone behind me, I saw a thick wall of fog. I felt like I was in a terrifying nightmare. I jumped through the mist with Leo in my hand, Franchesca, Gordock, and Raphael following swiftly behind. I landed with a thud into a soft, warm patch of sand. Leo landed next to me and I saw Franchesca along with Raphael and Gordock transported next to us.

"Just what in the name of dragon shit was that?!" I shouted, hitting the sand as I stood up and brushed it off me. Leo laughed along with Franchesca, but Raphael was silent. I looked at him sheepishly. "No offense Raphael, but I have never seen anything like that. And just where are we?" I asked, looking at the map.

"I am not really here, I am at the castle sipping tea and eating pastry." Leo said, standing up to study the map with me. He brushed himself off. "Well Mr. Wizard, where to next? Are we still on our planet? Did I eat something that is making me hallucinate? Perhaps it was the dwarves or the warrior women, they fed us something poisonous!" Leo joked, smiling at me.

"Oh, shut up you buffoon! We are on the right track. I do not know what that was, but I will get this sword even if I have to go through Sceptor's anus!" I exclaimed, pointing at where we were. "See, The map says we are in the Desert of Fears."

"The title does not sound like another *welcoming* place, my friend." Leo remarked sarcastically, baring his teeth.

"Well, I do not believe any of these places are *welcoming* us with bread and wine, Leo." I said to him, snapping the map shut. The sun was harsh and blinding here. All I saw were waves of sand that appeared to stretch off for eternity. Was I dreaming all of this? "I wonder why it's called Desert of Fears?" I asked. "According to the map, we must pass through the desert and past the three gates to Massimilla. Then, we set off through there and onward to Castle Enigma to the easternmost edge of the land. Nebula... must be... there."

I continued to think about it as I walked along the dry sand. We were all growing thirsty and tired. Raphael beat his wings frantically, but he still could not fly. The sun weakened us severely and as we walked we began to see faltering illusions that appeared and dissolved with the passing of each gust of dry wind. For hours we wandered the desert, leading us through an expanse of sandy dunes that stretched ever further as we walked.

"We are never going to get off this damn wasteland!" Leo shouted desperately at the sky.

"Calm down Leo, we *will* get there! If my blood should gush from my veins, we shall get there! I am not turning back. We must find the three Gates to Massimilla!" I declared. As I turned forward, a massive structure like a shadow appeared in the distance.

"That must be it! Leo! Look, there is the first gate!" I yelled, running toward it. Franchesca ran with me while Leo stood in disbelief. "I told you we would get here!" I exclaimed. As I approached, I saw that the first gate was a hulking structure made out of stone that towered high into the sky. I touched the gate's rough surface and looked up at it. In the center was a thin layer of transparent liquid, rippling like water in the wind. The land beyond could be seen through it, but when I stretched out my arm through the thin layer, it disappeared.

"All right, the Gods only know what is beyond this gate. I will go first and then all of you will follow behind me, one by one. Do we all understand this?" I said, looking at them. I saw them nod their heads and I turned to face the gate. I slowly put my hand through it and then my body. Turning back, I could still see my friends. I had reached the other side of the Gate. "This is nothing special! Come on! It's all right." I assured them. Leo then stepped forward, along with Franchesca and Raphael.

"This is nothing; it is the same as the other side." Franchesca said. I nodded to her remark and began walking straight ahead. I could see the other gate far away from us. I headed toward it when Ariaus appeared in the sand. My heart skipped a beat as I suddenly froze with terror. Did he follow us all this way? Was he already ahead of us? How did he get here? I ran after him so I could see him better. It was him! I stared at his pale skin and he gazed back with a smile on his face.

"Ah, my little angel. Where have you been? I have been waiting for you." he said with his soft voice.

"Kain! What are you doing?" Leo yelled to me. I looked at Leo and then ignored him, falling to my knees in front of Ariaus.

"Master... why are you doing this? Why did you murder my mother!? How could you be so cruel!?" I asked with tears in my eyes and tugging on the hems of his breeches.

"You must give yourself to Sceptor and serve him. That is your destiny, my child." He explained soothingly to me, touching my face with his soft fingertips. He knelt down with me and kissed my cheek. "I love you Kain, I have always loved you. Now is your time to show your power and take your place on the throne. Do not let these mortals turn you into something you are not. You can be more powerful than any God. Who needs your brother when you can have his castle and the entire world! Come with me, Kain. Come with me and rule this world as the most powerful being in all the universe."

I stared at him. I tried to open my mouth to speak, but my muscles seized. He was overpowering me. My Gods, has Sceptor used Ariaus to take over my body? Has Sceptor won? I continued to stare at Ariaus. *No! I will not allow you to do this to me! No!* I thought to no avail. He released his psychic grip on me with a lurch from his wrists. He laughed as I pushed him away and pulled out my sword. I swung my sword right through him and he disappeared. My hair wafted freely in the wind while the tears dripped down my cheek. *Where did he go?*

I felt a grip on my shoulder and I quickly turned around and thrust my sword into dense flesh. As hot blood trickled down my blade and onto my arm, I spied silky black hair and shocked green eyes and realized what I had done. I stabbed Leo! My eyes opened wide and I screamed, "Leo! NO! Dear Gods! What have I done!?" I fell to the ground in tears, holding him in my arms. I held Leo and sobbed until I heard my name.

"Kain... Kain... are you all right?" I looked around and saw nothing. I looked up and saw a woman that looked like a Goddess staring down at me. She was beautiful with her curly, blonde, hair flowing in the breeze. I was crying and rocking back and forth with Leo in my arms.

"I did not mean to do it. It... it was an accident. I am a monster!" I yelled.

"You must understand that none of this is real, Kain. Your father is watching you... Kain..." The woman said with her gold robe and blonde hair. I opened my eyes and heard my name again.

"Kain! Wake up!" Someone said while shaking me. I saw myself sitting in the sand and when I turned, I saw Leo. He was desperately trying to wake me up from that terrible nightmare. I could not keep up with what was going on. Did I hallucinate the entire time? Was Ariaus nothing but a vision? I never killed Leo? I jumped up from the ground and hugged him, then kissed him on his lips passionately.

He pulled me away and whispered, "Kain, what is wrong with you? You were screaming hysterically to yourself. I could not get you to stop. We have to get out of here quickly. This place can drive someone mad," Leo said, pulling me towards the second gate.

"I know now why they call this place Desert of Fears." I remarked, looking at Leo. "My fear is losing you! I saw a vision... I thought you were gone... but here you are." I sighed with relief.

"You know I will never leave you, Kain, and even if I'm gone, my spirit will fly beside you forever. Now let's get out of this place!" he said, pulling me to the front of the gate. The second Gate had two horned, scowling, demonic statues on either side. I looked around and felt Leo pull my arm, still holding my hand. I quickly began to run with him to the last gate that was even more hulking than the others. Before entering the final one, I saw the image of my father approach. My eyes widened; this man that passed away years ago was walking before my eyes. I tugged on Leo's hand and told him what I saw as the image drew me. I desired to run up to him and embrace him, but Leo held me tighter as I tried to spring forward.

"Father!" I called for him as I reached forward. Leo stopped me

"Kain, that is not your father. Your father is dead! Listen to me! This place shows us our fears and tricks us!" He shouted, his voice slowly fading as he spoke. I was lost in the figure before me who was coming close. I could see my father's long blonde hair and his mustache that covered much of the top of his lip. He had a smile on his face and he was dressed in the finest embroidered silk. I felt myself fall to the ground. When I looked up and opened my eyes, I was no longer in the desert. Instead, I was in a dewy forest. Leo slapped my face and shook me. "Kain? Are you all right?" he asked over and over.

"Yes, yes I am all right, Leo. Thank you. I was almost lost again in another hallucination. I wish I never went into this desert." I said, holding onto Leo and shaking my head.

"Where is everyone?" I asked softly in Leo's ear. At that moment out of nowhere, Franchesca and

Raphael flew from the sky and landed on the grassy ground. I saw them get up slowly and scratch their heads. "Are you two all right?" I asked kindly. They nodded and moaned in pain. I looked at Leo and got up from the ground.

"We must have been tossed through a series of portals within the gates. I never believed they were real up until now. From here, we need to find that damn Castle Enigma." I exclaimed, making a fist with my right hand. I hoped that we did not have to go through any portals like this again. I looked around to see whether or not we were back in our world. There were trees surrounding us like any forest, but the Gods knew where we could be. The visions messed with my head and now I could not get them out of my thoughts. I was terrified to go on to the next step. I did not want to go through anything like that again. I took Leo's hand and started walking through the woods. I noticed the sun was starting to go down; flashes of orange and purple glimmered from the sky and peeked through the tree tops. I looked down again at the map and saw that the woodland road of Massimilla stopped at a lonely castle at the edge of the worn page.

Will he try to destroy me? Will he think I wished trouble upon the world? I thought of what my brother would say when he saw me at the end of the journey. My mind was swinging back and forth. I could not keep it still from thoughts. These were the moments when I wish I could not think of anything at all.

Chapter Thirteen
Castle Enigma

After walking for two days in the woods, Leo spotted a castle off in the distance. I noticed Raphael had been quiet since we began to decipher and follow the map. As I was walking towards the castle, I felt warm fur brush up against my leg. I looked below me to see Franchesca purring softly.

I smiled down at her and she said to me, "My prince, I hope the sword will change me back."

I smiled and whispered, "I hope so too, my dear." She licked my hand gleefully as a response. I continued walking and nearly tripped over many of the large rocks that stuck out from the soil below us. We were coming close to the castle; as it faded into sight in the distance, it glowed with purple mist. The castle was huge; its walls and towers stretched high into the sky. The front facade was decorated with elaborate relief sculptures of angels, demons, dragons, and unicorns as if their images protected the castle. Large, dark birds circled high above the arched rooftops. The setting sun cast vivid light in pink, orange, and purple upon the face of the building. This place was beautiful, but dark in the same manner. I walked up to the main doors and studied the beautiful gold and silver carvings. This place told a story, but I could not decipher it. Everyone was behind me, watching to see what I would do. Despite the enormity of the castle, the doors only fit Leo, Franchesca, Gordock, and I. I looked at Raphael quizzically.

"I will be too large to go in there; I'll wait outside," Raphael exclaimed. I turned and nodded at him.

"That is all right, my friend. Leo, Gordock, and Franchesca will come with me. Are you two ready?" I asked, breathing heavily. Leo and Franchesca nodded and came closer to me. After turning and opening the door slowly, I grabbed a torch that rested by the side of the door and lit it with a flick from my wrist. We then entered the castle. The halls were dark and vast inside. I lit the path ahead with the torch and saw paintings on the walls and ceiling as I passed by, my two companions following close behind and the raven on my shoulder. There were torches on the walls of the castle. I lit each one as we walked through the hall and into a grand room with black marble flooring and a massively large fireplace. The fire was lit, meaning someone was already here.

I listened for noises that any mortal could make and I thought I heard a voice, although I couldn't gauge whether they came from below or above. The castle was so large that the sounds echoed just about anywhere. I walked in the middle of the large room and held my torch up to see if I could see further without having to move closer. The sounds of footsteps echoed ever louder. Leaning in, I saw torches and men holding them. They wore the colors from my brother's court. In was unmistakable; they were his knights.

I stared at them all and asked, "What is going on?" They held their swords up to us and as I was about to draw my weapon, I saw my brother walk through the soldiers to approach me.

"*Well, well, well...* if it is not my *brother* who wishes death upon me and the world," he said with a grin, moving my sword gently down with his slender fingers.

"My brother, I am not here to harm you or the world, but to save it and you! Please... believe me..." I started, but was cut off by Abel.

"Do *not* tell me such *filthy* lies! You sicken me as you speak, *Kain*. You are nothing to me anymore," He said with complete hatred in his voice.

"*No!* Prince Abel, please believe him. He is truly here to help," Leo insisted, walking closer to Abel. I saw the way he looked at my brother. Leo did not look at him the same way he looked at me.

"Ah, *Leo* speaks and wishes me to *believe*. I think *not*. Do you wish to *kill* me as well, my *trustful* knight that I thought was there to *protect* me? What did my *monstrous* brother do to you?" Abel inquired, touching Leo's face softly. I put my sword away and grabbed Abel's hand.

"Abel, please believe me. It is not *I* who wishes to harm you or the world. It is Ariaus!" I said, kissing his hand and holding it. He pulled his hand away and looked at me with disgust.

"Ariaus? How *dare* you speak of him that way! He is the only one who has been helping us track you down and stop you from getting the sword. He *knew* how to find the blade and *knew* you were going to use it for *evil*. You also captured my most *trusted* knight, *Leo* because you thought he would protect me if you tried to kill me. You put a spell on him to follow you. As to my perspective, everything seemed just as Ariaus told it. So the only one I *see* doing wrong is *you* and if you were not here to get the sword and destroy me, than *why* are you here?" He asked, staring into my eyes. I was speechless and could hardly breathe. I felt like I could say nothing to make him believe. Leo was even speechless. I had to tell him the truth and make him believe.

"I came to get the sword so I can stop Ariaus from harming you and making me work for Sceptor. And I did not capture Leo, nor did I put a *spell* on him. You must understand that Ariaus works for Sceptor and will stop at *nothing* to make him possess me with his evil desire." I said with sad, but serious eyes. He stared at me for an entire minute and then walked up to Leo.

"Did he capture and put a spell on you?" Abel asked, touching Leo's face again.

"I was never captured by Kain. Instead, he saved my life from a pack of wolves. I heard he was going to find this sword so he can save you and the world from Ariaus and Sceptor. I decided that I would help him. I was never captured or had any spell cast upon me by Kain." Leo said earnestly. Abel shook his head in disbelief.

"I *see* what happened to you now." Abel sighed, leaning forward to Leo's ear and whispering, "You fell in *love* with him, didn't you?" Abel then moved away, grinning.

"I... I did. He is a good and honest man. You are his brother and you can't even believe him!" Leo shouted. Abel stared at him, blinking his eyes as if he were shocked at how his former knight was acting. Abel walked up to me and touched my hair that hung over my shoulders and bangs and covered my dark eyes. From the shadows, Ariaus' aged form strolled directly behind my brother and touched his shoulder. Abel smiled at me and then turned to Ariaus. He dropped to his knees and kissed his hand. I watched him do this, how it seemed as if it was *I* making those actions. A sick feeling rose from the depths of my stomach.

"Dear Abel, I see you found your brother just as I suspected. As you see, I was right and you can even feel his *evil* gushing out from his *soul*. If *I* were *you*, I would destroy him before anything else," Ariaus said with his deep, velvet, soothing voice. I was shocked at what he was saying and how his eyes were those of a true demon. How could my brother who was blessed with the light of Vertigo believe such a cruel man? I thought in this moment that the sword could change my brother from good to evil. Even with such love in his heart, perhaps Ariaus could still bring some malice into him. Ariaus wished to kill me now so that he could use my brother.

Abel laughed and waved his hand for his knights to take me away. Leo and Franchesca were gripped and held down by the brutes. I pulled out my sword and began to strike at some of them, though I hesitated; how could I hurt my brother's knights? I let them take me like a fool. Gordock flew frantically toward the ceiling and disappeared into the darkness above. The men then dragged me into a large room filled with candles. They were lit with an eerie glow everywhere in the room. There were so many candles that it looked like the stars in the sky, enchanting and mysterious. I was placed up upon a massive, golden pentagon that rose upright from the floor. Mere feet in front of me was an altar with a beautiful sword resting in a golden sheath. *This must be Nebula,* I thought. I struggled to break free, but the men bound my limbs to each corner of the structure with gilded chain, my neck secured tightly at the top. I saw my brother walking up to me and stared at me with his beautiful eyes that appeared soulless. I could not believe this was the brother I knew. I could hear Leo trying to fight off the men that held him.

"Abel, do not do this. You cannot allow the evil to overpower you! Believe me when I say Ariaus is not helping you. Please *hear* me, my brother!" I screamed to him, unable to move any part of my body. Ariaus bellowed out with laughter from deep within his gut.

"Take the sword, Abel. Take the *sword* and *kill* him with it before he tries to get away. There is not much time! You hold the *power* now and there is nothing that can stop you. Do it! *Now*!" My former master ordered as he watched my brother take the sword from its golden casing. The sword was encrusted with purple jewels at the hilt, which was tipped in crystal of the same color and detailed in brilliant gold. The metal of the sword was polished and emitted an enchanting light. How fitting it looked in my brother's hands. He looked like a true king with such a massive and ornate sword. I stared at him with it and began to remember what he was going to do now that the weapon was in his hands.

"*NO*! Do not harm him, Abel! Please don't kill him! *Please...*" Leo begged with tears streaming down his cheek. I watched my brother walk up to me slowly with the sword. His eyes were dark and his expression was unreadable. He looked possessed. He laughed as he held the blade up to my chest. He slowly moved the tip and pressed it against my heart, which beat furiously while my mind raced. *How could he do this to me? Was he possessed by Sceptor? Could Sceptor have taken over his love and filled it with hatred and a lust for power? Have I forgotten the words of my father? How could I allow this to happen?*

"No, my brother! *Please*!" I said staring at him with tears dripping down my cheek. I needed to show him love as he did for me. I struggled to send him my message telepathically. *We must believe in love and forget the power. Then, Sceptor will not be able to overpower us. If he kills me, he will shed blood on the sword and he will be taken by Sceptor. Just as our father once said,* "Your brother loves you and you must love him back." *That is the secret to stopping Sceptor from overpowering the world with his evil. Love is the way to freedom from the malicious God and I feel as if it is too late to let you know this.* I opened my eyes to see the old woman from the woods appear in the room with Gordock on her shoulder.

"*Stop this at once*! Children, what are you doing? Abel, dear boy, you cannot continue *this*!" She insisted. I was so overjoyed and relieved to see her.

"Shut up old woman, you know nothing of what is happening. I demand you to leave this place or you too will *perish* with my *devilish* brother." Abel ordered, looking back at me with a grin on his face, his bangs falling in front of his eyes. *Who was the devilish one?* "Now my *brother*, you will taste the metal of this sword, followed by your own *blood*." Abel said, moving over to my cheek and kissing it.

I felt a sharp pain jabbing into my heart. *My Gods, he forced the sword into my chest! How could he do this to me*? I stared at him with my mouth open and blood slowly pouring from the wound. It gushed from my heart and dripped down my clothing. My brother stared at me, no longer with a grin. He looked shocked at what he did. My blood was on his face and in his hands. Again I felt a sharp pain, but worse. He slid the sword from my heart and I nearly passed out from the continuous pain that seemed to stop my breathing. My vision was getting blurry and I felt as if I could not speak.

"My *Gods*, what have I done?" Abel whispered softly to himself in shock.

"You *killed* your brother who was going to *slay* you, *dear boy*." Ariaus said, touching my brother's shoulder. Abel stared at me with watery eyes. My consciousness was fading; I was slowly dying.

I have failed you, father. Will you ever forgive me? I thought desperately, *Will my soul be given to Sceptor or Vertigo? What will become of me now and what of Leo? What of Franchesca, the old woman, Mandel, and Raphael? I never helped Franchesca get her human form back. I promised her I would. I have failed everyone and even myself. Is this my destiny?* I then closed my eyes and saw nothing but darkness and had the sensation of floating away. *Is this where you go when you die? Where are the Gods and Goddesses?* I pondered.

I then thought I saw a small light in the distance. I wanted to reach it, so I tried hard to push myself there. *Was I really moving myself or did I only think I was*? This was a strange feeling. Though I had no body, I still thought I had one. I was lost. However, I was reaching this light; I did it well. As I got closer, I saw what was inside; I saw my father standing there and watching me. He waved to me with a smile on his face. I got closer to him and I felt that I could stand with him in a sunlit plain, feeling grass between our toes. Our surroundings were bright and glowed with a glimmering light. This place was not filled with hate or power, but rather, with love and warmth. I felt my father hug me, though I had no idea how with no body. He was still in human form. *Was I*? I kissed his cheek and though his mouth was not moving, I could hear him speak.

"My son, you are filled with the light of Vertigo. He will make sure that you fulfill your true destiny to save the world from Sceptor. You *must* go back and do this. I am with you, my son. *Now go...*" He said to me, showing expression, but no words from his mouth. I did the same to him.

"No father, I do not want to go back... I am here now and my body is not strong enough to stop the God of darkness. I do not *want* to go back... *please...* father..." I said, feeling like I was crying, but knowing it was just habit from when I had a body. I was sucked back away from the light and the warmth and the feeling of love and no pain, back through the darkness and the cold to where my body lay in agony-induced paralysis. I opened my eyes and felt a worse pain than when I was stabbed. Sharp pangs shot up and around my body. I did not want to come back.

"*No, send me back! I want to go back*!" I screamed. I opened my eyes while spitting up blood and trying to wriggle loose from the chains. My brother was below me on one knee reading the letter my father had written to me. I saw him holding the pieces of the letter, thought of our father, and began to cry. *Father... why did you let this happen to me? I want to be with you*! I cried while weeping with tears of blood. Leo looked up from sobbing and saw I was still alive. He wrenched himself from the men that held him. He ran up to me and kissed me on my lips. I stared at him and it seemed all my pain left my body for one second.

"*Leo...*" I whispered. My brother stood up and my former master turned to see me in shock.

"*What*?! He was *dead*!" Ariaus screeched, drawing closer to me. The old woman then ran as quickly as she could up to Ariaus and stopped him from coming any closer.

"You stop *right* there, *you monster*!" She demanded. Something strange suddenly happened to her. A light began to shine through her body as if to break itself free. The shine grew so strong that all of us had to turn our heads and look away. A song began to fill the room like an angel's melody with soft drums. I was overcome by a safe, nurturing feeling. The old woman was no longer a crone, but a Goddess. I was captivated by her as she floated close to me. Caring not to see what everyone else was doing, I focused on her alone.

She placed her white hand gently on my chest. I closed my eyes and felt an intense heat strike my heart. She slowly pulled her hand away and I looked up to see her face. Her hair was a pure gold that hung down in curls and she was wearing a long golden dress. She was shimmering with gilded color along with her eyes and face, which shined in radiant platinum. She seemed made of the precious metal; how beautiful she looked. It was hard to believe that she was in fact once an old hag.

"*Looks* are not always what they seem. Isn't that right, my prince?" she asked with a rich and echoing voice that emitted to and from all parts of the room. The candles were glowing brighter and everyone was staring at her, motionless. The knights bowed their heads and knew that this was a Goddess that worked for Vertigo. She beamed at me kindly, light bouncing radiantly off of her face. The sword was then magically pulled from my brother's hand, glided through the air, and was placed in the grip of the Goddess. She turned to me and used her mind to break the chains that bound me to the pentagon.

I fell to the ground and she floated down to me. She gently took my hand and gave me the sword. I stared at her and I began to hear a beautiful and soft Celtic melody, as if sang by the angels. The drums beat harder and everything else was quiet, but the music began to rise in my heart. The angels sang and the light grew brighter.

"You are the one who holds the heart of gold, now you hold the sword made from such a heart." She said as the sword was placed in my hand. I felt its power and its love and knowing now how to wield and what to use it for. I stood up and heard the drums beat harder and with a more enchanting rhythm. I pointed it at my brother and grinned. He stared up at me as he was on the ground, holding my father's letter. He feared me and felt he was going to die.

I placed the blade under his chin and smiled. "Stand up my brother, join me with Vertigo and leave the power of Sceptor. We can both stop him by using our most precious gift," I said softly to him.

He stood up and whispered, "What gift is that, my brother?"

"The gift of love," I replied. He smiled at me and nodded. I saw that warm glow now begin to come back into him. The darkness that surrounded him was now gone. My old brother was back. For once in our lives, we both looked so much alike that we even both glowed with the same shade of light. I looked over at the goddess and behind her, a large portal of light opened up. Behind her was a shadow, a human form and I noticed it was my father. My eyes widened.

"You did good, Kain, and your name shall be remembered forever as well as your brother, Abel. I will see you two soon in time, but for now, I love you both and shall be watching over you. Farewell and may the light of Vertigo be with you," my father said, waving to us both and I felt a few tears drip down my cheek. I saw another shadow of a woman that looked in the distance like mother. When she came closer, I noticed it was in fact her and she smiled at us both. She hugged my father and they both beamed happily at us. How beautiful she looked with her long, blond, braided hair. She was wearing the most beautiful dress with long, billowing sleeves. She waved as the light began to get smaller and the goddess of gold began to fade with that light. My brother and I both stood there in tears and still watched where the light was before it faded. Leo came running up to me and kissed me passionately. I kissed him back and then hugged him tightly.

"I love you Leo," I whispered in his ear and I heard him say the same back to me. He was crying on my shoulder. I slowly moved away from him and smiled. I looked at my brother and saw him stare at me, ashamed and yet happy I was alive. I pulled him close to me and embraced him. He began to weep as well and I held him very tightly.

"I love you, Abel. I love you," I said softly to him.

"I am sorry my brother, I do not know what came over me... I... please believe me, my brother," he said.

I whispered softly back, "I believe you... I believe you." I rocked him side to side. I slowly pulled away from him and walked over to Ariaus. "I want you to leave from our sights and never return. I do not care where you go, but do not ever show your face to us again. If I see you, then I shall destroy you. That I make a promise to myself. Now go and leave us!" I demanded. Ariaus stared at me and then bowed his head. He slowly turned and walked away. I walked up to my brother and as I got closer to him, I noticed Franchesca was by his side. I smiled at her and walked up to her.

"Did you save the world yet, my prince?" she asked, laughing to herself.

I laughed with her and whispered, "Yes my dear, so it seems." I placed the sword gently on her head and thought of her as she used to be. When I opened my eyes, I saw her raven black hair and her forest green eyes, shimmering like emeralds, not as a cat, but as a beautiful woman. I smiled at her and my brother took his cloak off to wrap around her. She smiled back at me and hugged me.

"Thanks to you Kain, you have kept your promise, found my lost love, Morilda which was unexpected, and returned me to my true form, a warrior woman. And yes, that's right, I was once one of them. I belonged to their tribe long ago until I was cursed by the witch and ever since then; I lost touch of my female companions and stayed at the tower never to see

Morilda and my fellow warriors again. Now that you have returned me to myself, I shall be by the side of my Queen, my leader, and my love." She said, leaning in close and whispered softly with her hot breath against my cheek. "Thank you..." Franchesca kissed my soft skin and then my lips. She threw herself on me and wrapped her arms tightly around my waist. I then laughed and lifted her off the ground. I was so happy that I began to cry.

"What a wonderful day this turned out to be. Today will always be remembered and every year of this date, there shall be a feast. I call this the Feast of The Lost Sword Nebula!" I declared, holding up the sword. Everyone cheered and held up their swords. As we walked out of the castle, I heard a raven. It was Gordock and he landed on my shoulder. I began to laugh along with my brother, Leo, and Franchesca.

"Ha…where have you been, my friend?" I said laughing softly to myself. I looked up and noticed Raphael stared down at us.

"What did I *miss*? I heard all *kinds* of noise and saw bright lights. What happened?" Raphael asked. All of us began to laugh.

"It is a long story, my friend. I will tell you over a large fire and a feast." I said, still laughing to myself. Raphael smiled and asked us if we wanted a lift; the air was light and clear, fitting for flight, and it carried a sweet scent.

"Of course, my friend. We would love a lift," I replied. We climbed up on Raphael and I saw my brother on the ground. "Would you like to join us, my brother? It is a lot of fun..." I asked him. He just smiled and looked at his men who were walking over to a large ship in the distance that was once covered by purple mist.

Abel then looked back at us and said, "I guess it would not harm my men if I went with you instead of them. Excuse me while I inform them." He walked over to his knights and told them what he was doing. My brother then ran back to us and jumped up on the dragon's back. I was in front; Leo was behind me, then my brother, and Franchesca. Gordock flew beside us. We flew for hours and watched the sun go down, creating the most beautiful colors against the clouds. My brother was enjoying himself immensely. I wished this day would never end, but I knew it would and so would the next and the next.

"What will we do when we get back to the castle, Kain?" Abel asked me.

"What will we do? We will have a feast!" I said, laughing softly. "I'm starving and I haven't eaten in days! And of course, a bath would be lovely," I added.

"But then, what do we do tomorrow?" Abel asked, laughing. I bowed my head and chuckled with him.

"We will do what we were destined to do, and that is... rule the kingdom together, spreading peace and justice throughout the world," I replied, knowing that this was not the end, but rather, the beginning. I held The Lost Sword Nebula, which was no longer lost at last, but found.

Ginger Anne London is the author of *Kain* and soon to be many new titles in the fantasy and sci-fi genres. She lives in the United States with her fiancée and has been writing novels for thirteen years.

www.ingramcontent.com/pod-product-compliance
Lightning Source LLC
LaVergne TN
LVHW050631100826
845148LV00011B/1827
9780615734590